CHERRY'S JUBILEE

BY

V. J. DEVEREAUX

Erotic Romance by V. J. Devereaux
The Book of Demons series
Demon's Kiss
Demon's Embrace

Cooking Class
Special Delivery

The Bound series
Blood Bound
Magic Bound

Discover titles by Valerie Douglas

Fantasy
The Coming Storm series
The Coming Storm
A Convocation of Kings
Not Magic Enough
Setting Boundaries

Song of the Fairy Queen

The Servant of the Gods series
Servant of the Gods
Heart of the Gods

Romance
The Millersburg Quartet
Dirty Politics
Directors Cut
Irish Fling
Two Up

Lucky Charm
Picture Perfect

Dedication

To my friend Gary, your cheerful presence and enthusiast encouragement are missed.

to Rusty — silly dog, you were such a character, there was nothing you wouldn't eat, but you weren't supposed to catch the cars you chased

Chapter One

"I want a truly decadent dinner, people, knock their socks off,
Connor O'Donnell said." Patrick grinned wickedly. "So, we're
going to knock their socks off. He wants decadent, we'll give him
decadent. With your help, Cherry, we're going to give him a
dessert he'll never forget."

Connor O'Donnell was finally taking over as CEO of his
family company, O'Donnell International. Although there were
some members of the Board of Directors who might object, he'd
decided to celebrate with a lavish party that included his two best
friends and a select group of his peers. It would be a party people
would talk about for years, if not decades. The reward for the most
decadent contribution would be a contract as executive chef with
O'Donnell International. As a favor to her friend Patrick, one of the
best dessert chefs in the city, Cherry had given him a heads up. She
just hadn't expected to be quite so involved.

Or so excited by what Patrick had in mind.

Letting out a breath, Cherry looked at what Patrick had done
so far and had to admit she was both impressed and astonished.

Around the interior of the commercial refrigerator were
several life size statues of the front of the female torso done in
various flavors of chocolate. Cherry had a little difficulty believing
that those forms had been made from her, despite remembering
vividly Patrick coaxing her into position — bent slightly backward
over a hassock — before painting the silicone on her to prepare the
mold.

Patrick had one last piece to prepare but as it was the pièce de
résistance and had special requirements, it had to be left until last.

Shaking her head, she looked around at the completed pieces.

"They look incredible, Patrick," Cherry said. "Just amazing. If
you don't get the job after this, the man is insane."

Patrick beamed. "They do look amazing, if I do say so myself,
at least partly thanks to you, Cherry, my sweet."

Insane or not, Connor O'Donnell was also incredibly hot, tall, dark and handsome with blue eyes in a strong Irish face. He was also, to Patrick's regret and despite his long-term committed relationship to his beloved Alan, as straight as they came. It was a damn shame and a waste as far as he was concerned. The man was simply gorgeous with all that thick dark, curling hair and those laser blue eyes.

And that body…

Gay Patrick might be, but he knew what straight men wanted and if Connor O'Donnell wanted decadent he intended to give it to him in spades. What Patrick wanted was that job in corporate headquarters as executive chef. Then he and Alan could move to a better apartment, maybe even a house. One with a decent kitchen.

What he had in mind might get that job for him. He was just glad Cherry had given him the inside scoop about it and was willing to help out, especially given what he had in mind.

"We're not done yet, Cherry. Just wait. All right," he said, "Now, we're going to have to tie you down in the proper position to set the stage and secure you in place to keep you from moving. Even an inch and it'll all be ruined. Plus, we want the right effect, don't we, Alan?"

He winked at his partner, who just grinned.

Not for the first time, Cherry had a moment of second thoughts, mixed with a burst of anticipation. *Was she really going to do this*? It had seemed like fun, sexy, and a bit of a rush when Patrick had first suggested it.

Of course, now wasn't exactly the time to back out. Especially since she would be the centerpiece, the pièce de résistance, an exciting idea in itself. She couldn't, wouldn't, let Patrick down like that.

Besides she'd agreed to do it…and there was still something incredibly exciting and sexy about it, too. Connor O'Donnell wasn't the only one who liked things a little decadent. Cherry had always been a bit of an exhibitionist, something she kept carefully hidden — a contradiction in terms but there you go.

This would definitely be both decadent and exhibitionist.

Besides, just the thought made her a little hot. No, it was making her a lot hot.

With a shrug and a grin, Cherry let the little robe she wore against the iciness of the refrigerator fall and took Alan's offered hand. The cold chilled her nipples, tightening them.

Alan grinned impishly, his eyes twinkling as he helped Cherry up to the narrow platform raised above the main table beneath the statue in the dining area. He had signed on to this little adventure enthusiastically as soon as Patrick had mentioned it, loving the theatricality of it.

She settled into place, letting her head rest on the little pillow set there and got as comfortable as she could. The back was curved to arch her torso, and to provide a place to hide the ice that would keep her chilled.

Alan and Patrick got to work.

The two bound her to the table with red velvet cords at her wrists and ankles, securing her arms and legs into the positions Patrick wanted.

Cherry felt a little exposed and more than a little naughty, but it wasn't entirely uncomfortable. She'd been worried about that. Especially if she might have to spend hours that way, as seemed likely.

Letting out a breath that misted a little in the cool refrigerated air, Cherry nodded, grinning back as Alan brushed out her hair so it spilled over the table to conceal the prop for her head.

Alan set a little faux gold fillet across her forehead and into her hair just so. He and Patrick blew away any stray hairs with hair dryers on cool, before Patrick sprayed a light mist of sugar water over it like hair spray to keep it in place, scrunching it gently as he went, before sprinkling it with sugar sparkles as it dried to make it glitter and shine beneath the lights.

Once they had her tied into the proper position, Alan — a makeup artist on Broadway — set to work on her face as Patrick painted every inch of her skin with a coating of honey, shaking sugar sparkles and raw sugar over it so every inch of her body would gleam and glisten.

While he was gay Patrick knew what straight men liked. Cherry had a body to die for, just perfect for this little exhibition with big full breasts, a waistline she worked hard to keep trim, a tight butt and killer legs. She also had a lovely face, a warm heart and a willingness to try almost anything at least once.

Like this.

What he couldn't figure out was why some man hadn't snatched her up.

With a little bit of luck though and a little help, he thought, with a private grin, *this might just do it*. He had his own plans. What Cherry didn't know wouldn't hurt her. And he had his suspicions on that.

If nothing else, this would definitely get Connor O'Donnell's attention.

Patrick glanced at the clock nervously but made himself keep working patiently and steadily.

Eyeing her, her position and what they had done with her, Patrick nodded in satisfaction as he and Alan quickly set out the rest of the display.

Once again Cherry asked herself if she was really going to do this? There was a remote chance that something more, something else might happen… It was a remote chance, but a chance all the same.

Patrick wasn't the only one who thought Connor O'Donnell was hot. She had secretly lusted for the man from the moment she had joined the company. She also liked and admired him. He had bucked the Board of Directors. One of the first things he had done when he'd been named CEO was to raise the wages the Board had convinced his father to keep stagnant.

Connor's two friends Jed and Erik were just as gorgeous in their own way. She certainly wouldn't have kicked any of their shoes out from under her bed.

The rumor was the three were inseparable friends but just how inseparable were they? Her heart fluttered at the thought.

It would be interesting. Some would say insane. She grinned at the thought. She loved a challenge. Nerves and excitement had kept her from eating all day.

It was more than a little sensual and erotic to be prepared this way — the sensation of having the honey poured over every inch of her naked body, even parts of her most intimate areas — by anyone. Her whole body felt charged. She had showered before she came but even so they had sprayed her body clean before they even started to make certain she was pristine everywhere, both inside and out. Alan had even trimmed the tight curls between her legs.

Bags of ice were hidden beneath the tablecloth under her to keep her body chilled while they worked and for the first few moments of the presentation. It was working very well. She was freezing, but not to the point of shivering…yet.

Patrick had given her very explicit instructions.

It was a good thing they had tied her down. As he drizzled her legs with an intricate tracery of chocolate it tickled. It took a monumental effort of will on her part not to wiggle as the chocolate was run over her cooled skin, hardening as it touched.

"Close those pretty blue eyes, sweetie," Alan told her and sprayed her face lightly with sugar water, sprinkling raw sugar and glittery sprinkles over it as it dried so her skin looked glazed. He carefully painted her lips with cherry glacè so they were candied a deep red.

"Whatever you do, don't lick your lips," he cautioned.

There wasn't a single portion of her body you couldn't touch or lick and find to be sweet.

"Even if you open those beautiful baby blues," Patrick said, "no one would know you, Cherry."

Alan had done his magic, rimmed her eyes with dark gray liner, turning her eyes smoky and smoldering, almost Egyptian in appearance, and played up her high cheekbones with color.

It wasn't likely anyone there would recognize her anyway. You couldn't get much farther away from her pin-striped, buttoned down, tightly coifed corporate persona than this, especially without her glasses. The problem was that O'Donnell Corporation and Connor O'Donnell, particularly, very much needed that side of her, especially these days. It was too important people take her seriously in the office, but every now and then a girl needed to break out.

This would do it.

Cocking his head, Patrick nodded in approval. "Perfect. Now, hold still, darlin'."

She gasped as something thick and wet squirted over intimate parts of her….

"Just a little honey, sweetie," Patrick said, grinning. "For effect. In case someone looks. Or gets hungry."

Her breath caught at that thought. She gave him a look.

Unrepentant, Patrick just winked at her.

Cherry didn't dare shake her head at him, fighting not to laugh. He was incorrigible. He apparently had higher hopes than she did.

There was one last chocolate torso to put in place. The thinnest one yet.

It had taken more than a few tries to get the right consistency, so they could get it out of the flexible mold without breaking it. The other torsos were early tries that also helped add to the atmosphere.

Patrick had carefully adjusted and arranged this particular one for a specific purpose.

It had been altered so it cradled Cherry's beautiful breasts and pushed them upward a little to mound whitely above the dark brown chocolate, with her nipples at the very edge of the confection. He had gilded it with edible gold to emphasize the smooth muscles from which it had been molded. A carved strawberry rose was placed over each nipple. More honey was then applied to her breasts so it pooled between them.

That one couldn't be put into position until the last minute though or it would start to melt. That time had come.

It was cold in the freezer even with the door open and Cherry's nipples were as hard as small pebbles as a result when Patrick finally put the strawberries in place. And there was the anticipation.

A very light weight settled over her naked hips and Cherry looked carefully to see Patrick setting a foamy skirt of marzipan and spun sugar over them, settling it over her to match the angle of the mold from which it had been taken. The sticky honey held it in place.

Patrick dusted more sugar sparkles over her from head to toes.

The timing was getting short.

"Are you ready, Cherry, my sweet?" Patrick asked.

One of her best friends, Patrick was one of the few who knew this had been a fantasy of hers, to be put on display like this…and then there was what came after, if she was lucky.

Last chance to change her mind. Excitement, anticipation and a little apprehension raced through her.

She took a breath and nodded carefully.

Patrick turned. "Alan?"

His partner nodded.

They took her and the other torsos into the dessert room, unveiling the dry ice beneath the tables to keep the tables cool, the mist from it adding to the ambiance. Alan allowed the drapery on the tables to fall. Trays of fruit and cakes already awaited. Both men pulled on their tuxedo jackets. Patrick took his place as Alan went to the doors and threw them wide.

Chapter Two

So far the party was going very well, Connor thought, sipping a flute of excellent champagne as he wandered through the crowd. He had set a challenge to some of the most promising chefs and culinary wizards in the city, each to one task, their choice — to create a meal so decadent and enticing the magazines would write about it for years to come and no one who attended would ever forget it.

The reward for the most impressive and creative of them would be to become executive chef for O'Donnell International. A multi-billion dollar corporation with offices around the world, it was no small offer.

The chefs had risen to the occasion.

Already there had been a choice of appetizers, soup or salad, and the entrees and now finally, the dessert.

The appetizers had been fabulous, beginning with foie gras, a ceviche and a tapenade, progressing to filet mignon or gratinée de coquille St Jacques for the entree. Everyone had been advised to eat sparingly to leave room for the following course.

Each course was kept carefully separate, with entertainment from one of the best jazz bands in the city as they moved from one room to the next, from soup to salad to entrée to dessert, each presented by the chef who had prepared it.

All that remained now was the dessert and Patrick Monaghan had promised something truly spectacular.

Connor looked at Jedidiah and Erik, his two closest friends through high school — Connor's father following the pattern established by his own father and grandfather, who hadn't believed in private schools — and college, as well as corporate officers of O'Donnell International. They were his good right and left hands, the only two people he could really trust.

He pushed away the bitterness and anger.

Not tonight, he told himself firmly. Tonight, he would enjoy himself.

As his troubleshooter, his friend Jed balanced tact and diplomacy with the ability to shoot from the hip if necessary, while Erik was his new project coordinator — looking for opportunities to take the company in new directions. Neither had gotten his position just because they were his friends. Both had advanced degrees and shared his vision for the company, where it was going and where it should go.

Unlike others.

Given the difficulties he was having with the Board of Directors, he needed the help.

The Board had dragged their collective feet before officially naming him C.E.O. He wasn't his father and that's who they wanted. As much as he had loved the man, as C.E.O. his father had let the Board run him more than he had run it. That was going change, the Board knew it, didn't like it and he had no doubt they were trying to find ways around it.

Connor looked around at the people who gathered, laughing and talking.

For now, though he wouldn't think about it, he would concentrate on the evening.

Looking over the crowd, Jed lifted an eyebrow, "It's quite a party. Looks like you've got another success on your hands, Conn."

Eyeing some of the ladies passing by, Erik grinned. "They won't forget this for a while, that's for certain."

Connor hardly gave the women a passing glance. Corporate wife types, they were as straitlaced as they came in their designer dresses, their makeup a perfect mask, not a hair out of place, not an adventurous bone in their stick-thin bodies. In fact, that was true of most of the people here, including the few board members who had deigned to come. Two were supporters, while one was here to find fault, already counting the cost, Connor could see it in his eyes.

There were those both on and off the Board who considered him nothing more than a playboy — with some justification, he had to admit, considering his past. As long as they also ignored both his MBA and a master's degree in accounting as well as the time he'd spent working at all levels of the company.

Part of the purpose of this party, if he were to be honest, was defiance.

As his past had consisted of assuming his father would live to a ripe old age like his grandfather and great-grandfather and not die of an unexpected heart attack at the early age of fifty-one — leaving Connor to inherit the family business at thirty-one — Connor had spent much of the time when he wasn't working in the company's best interests having fun. Climbing mountains, racing cars and motorcycles, chasing women and generally carousing — most of it in the company of the two men beside him.

Some now expected him to settle down but the idea of settling down the way these people wanted him to horrified him.

He craved adventure, excitement and he wanted someone in his life who wanted those same things, someone who wouldn't mind taking off on a motorcycle jaunt on a whim in the near constant company of Jed and Erik. He wasn't letting go of his two best friends. No woman would come between them. It was a package deal. She would have to take them, too.

If they could find one, just one, woman like that, though, he'd marry her in an instant. There had to be at least one in the world but so far they hadn't found her.

The rest of those attending this event were clients — the rare and special few who might appreciate this kind of thing, people who appreciated adventure, a little daring, something exciting — and a few in business and from the society media. He wanted to make sure the world knew there was a new top gun at O'Donnell — and didn't forget it any time soon.

"There's one last course," Connor reminded his friends.

It would make or break the evening, leaving the final and most lasting impression—the one people would never forget.

Almost as if he had signaled for it, the final set of doors opened onto the last room, the dessert room.

A collective gasp of amazement escaped the small crowd as they passed through the doors.

Following, Connor had to admit even he was impressed.

The basic décor of the room was gold-veined black marble walls with a dark gray plush carpet. It had been transformed into something resembling an ancient Greek or Roman temple, with tall white faux-marble pillars set in stark contrast against the gleaming dark marble walls. Low tables and reclining couches were scattered around the room, the very picture of Greco-Roman decadence. Candles flickered in sconces on the walls.

Pan flutes played softly in the background, evocative and haunting. Candles scented the air.

Scattered around the room were three statues made out of chocolate, one each in white, milk, and dark chocolate, female torsos of perfect proportion, the breasts high, full and rounded, the nipples tight, just the way he liked them, the waist slender, muscled, the belly taut.

A mist of cool air spilled over and around them, to waft across the floor, lending a magical aura to the room.

The figures were nude, the one in white chocolate with the areola painted a light pink with cherry glace, the nipples tinted a little darker. Another, in dark chocolate, wore a lacy white filigree of spun sugar like a toga, leaving one full breast exposed. The last, the milk chocolate, wore nothing but a spangling of fruit from nipple height down to the thighs. A stream of liquid chocolate pooled just below the hips of each as if they were rising from an ocean of it, the flickering light of hidden pots of canned fuel beneath the molten chocolate dancing in the cool fog that floated around each torso. Gilded cornucopia of fresh fruit spilled their contents wantonly in a rainbow of colors across the tables. Little finger cakes were mixed among them — Patrick's signature desserts. Tiny cheesecakes, sacher torte, macaroons as light as air, creampuffs, mille Feuille were piled on plates everywhere. Little cups of crème brulee awaited a piece of fruit or a dip of chocolate. Glasses of champagne were scattered around, each with a raspberry, blueberry or a slice of strawberry in it.

That wasn't what caused the gasps though and Connor went hot and hard at the sight of what did. Jed nearly choked, and Erik came to a complete stop.

At the head of the room stood what appeared to be a white marble statue of the Greek god Zeus from the thighs up, in all his magnificent and rampant male glory, one hand reaching down and out toward the pièce de résistance…

It was the most magnificent and erotic thing Connor had ever seen. He had asked for decadent, but this was simply incredible and absolutely brilliant.

Spotlighted at Zeus's feet, splayed out across a table like an offering to the god, was what appeared to be a woman made of sugar and honey, her pale golden skin gleaming and sparkling in sharp contrast to the dark walls. Her head was angled slightly toward them, her sugared golden hair tumbled around it. She wore a thin breastplate of gilded chocolate from the full white mounds of her breasts down to her ribs. Strawberries stood at the top of the breastplate while a toga of spun sugar appeared to have either been pushed up her shapely legs to expose them or pushed down to spill around her hips. A tracery of chocolate laces ran up her legs to bind painted-on chocolate sandal ties. Between the breastplate and the foamy spun-sugar toga was a short expanse of bare skin, the dip of her navel and her toned stomach dripping honey.

Her fine-featured face was lovely, each line sparkling with sugar, her rosy mouth glistening, firm and perfectly shaped, her kohl-rimmed eyes closed. Honeyed arms draped gracefully down across the table below her. One knee was bent and cocked a little while the other draped seemingly loosely to the table below.

Each firmly muscled limb was secured with red velvet bonds.

Spilled around her was an array of fresh fruit and Patrick's little cakes for dipping in the honey dripping from each arm and leg, from the pool in the cup of her navel, between her gorgeous breasts, or from the gilded chocolate breastplate now slowly melting from the heat of her body.

She was beautiful, glorious, the defeated warrior queen offered as sacrifice to the God.

And to them.

The entire room erupted in applause as Connor, Jed and Erik made their way around her, shaking their heads incredulously.

As cameras flashed from cell phones, the light reflecting from the marble walls Connor had to applaud as well, bowing to Patrick in acknowledgement of his expertise and creativity before he turned to look around the room.

It was astonishing and beautiful.

With a slight bow, Patrick acknowledged the applause, gesturing Connor and his friends to the head table and the couches around it, raised on a dais for the perfect view of their guests and the centerpiece, his dark eyes knowing.

Curious, Connor dipped a strawberry in the pool of honey in the woman's concave stomach and swirled it around inside the cup of her navel. Scraping the fruit across her body was deliciously sensual, an incredibly erotic thing to do. He and Jed watched as Erik took a piece of pineapple and slipped it up the rounded swell of the side of her breast to gather the chocolate dripping there.

That alone had Connor going hard as he walked around the table admiring Patrick's creation.

Erik sucked the chocolate from the fruit before gliding it across her skin again.

Connor froze for a moment, his breath catching again as he realized the woman on the table had been cleverly angled to give one view to the majority of the room but another entirely to those at the head table and he hardened even further. One other thing quickly became apparent — she was utterly and completely nude beneath the confection.

His breath came a little short.

Jed caught sight of her, too, and took a breath, elbowing Erik to catch his attention as well.

"Conn," Jed said, quietly, his attention riveted. "Erik."

Nodding, Connor said, going hot and hard, "I saw."

Erik glanced over at them and followed the direction of their gazes. For a moment he paused, lifting an eyebrow and then he popped the piece of fruit into his mouth. He swallowed hard.

From this angle she looked seductively enticing, a little wanton with her legs spread enough to reveal a glimpse of her sex so it looked as if she was indeed an offering to the god, either anticipating him as a lover or as if he had just finished with her. It was an astonishingly erotic tableau.

Patrick stepped up alongside them.

"Her name is Cherry, really and truly, and she's a volunteer, not a professional," Patrick said quietly, stepping up alongside them. "However, if you'd like, you can help yourself to whatever you see. I'll leave you and your guests to enjoy your dessert."

Bowing, Patrick turned to leave, giving Cherry a wink.

She hardly noticed.

Connor went still. The invitation was clear. He looked at Jed and Erik and knew by the expression on Jed's face that he didn't have to say anything.

That particular sight was on Jed's personal top-ten list.

The view as far as Jed was concerned was incredible—light beads of golden honey were caught in the tight close-trimmed curls between her shapely white thighs, her sex lightly beaded with it as if with her own juices in anticipation of what was to come.

He loved pussy. He loved playing with it, he loved eating it, and she had one of the sweetest pussies, literally, that he'd ever seen.

Almost involuntarily, he reached between those parted legs to run a finger lightly between the plump, rosy, tender folds, her labia slick, raising it to his mouth to taste with a low groan. It was sweet, with a touch of her musk, the rich flavor of her arousal.

"Honey," he murmured, even as sucked it from his finger. She was wet and not just from the honey. He looked at Connor. "This is turning her on."

Just looking at her turned Jed on and he had a pretty good guess it was turning Connor and Erik on as well.

He had the strongest urge to lick the chocolate laces from one shapely leg, his tongue tracing the lines of it up along the tender skin on the inside of her thigh, gathering the chocolate up until he reached the very top. And then start working his way up the other leg.

If she would let him.

A faint murmur escaped from the woman and lovely long-lashed eyes as blue as the sky opened, her rich red lips parting a little on a gasp. She quivered just a little.

Beside him both Connor and Erik went still as a rush went through Jed at her sharp intake of breath… but no protest.

It had been impossible for Cherry not to gasp at the sudden and incredibly intimate touch, a rush of heat going through her nevertheless as a finger had slid up her slit. A sudden gush of warmth had rushed to her pussy, flooding it. Even so, as startling as it was, she forced herself to stay still.

But it surprised her into opening her eyes, to find Connor O'Donnell only a foot or so away, his friends Jed and Erik to each side of him, Jed standing closest to the table.

As the new CEO of O'Donnell International, Connor O'Donnell had made the papers and the news and entertainment channels, so it wasn't as if Cherry hadn't seen him before. But certainly not this close. Her only in-house encounter with him had been at a far greater distance than the TV gave her.

Cherry had been surreptitiously watching them all from beneath her lashes.

In a tuxedo Connor O'Donnell was gorgeous, sophisticated, elegant and controlled, his gaze watchful and reserved, a little cynical, but there were also stories of what he was like outside the office walls.

Cherry could appreciate that as she lived something of a dual life herself. She could also sympathize. The battle between him and the Board of Directors was common knowledge and from what she heard it threatened to get worse.

He was taller than she'd thought and much more handsome in person than when standing at a far-away podium.

Dark hair curled around his strong, sexy Irish face, his rare smile a little crooked, his eyes a brighter and more brilliant blue up close than they were at a distance. His shoulders were broad and strong, but he was narrower in the hips, even in the tailored tuxedo.

She couldn't help but wonder what he looked like with it off.

It was the force of his personality, though, mirrored in those incredibly intense blue eyes, that caught her, a sense of power, of energy, barely held in check.

Beside him were his two best friends, both handsome men in their own right.

The one with the light brown hair and soulful — according to the secretaries — long-lashed deep brown eyes in his slightly long face was Connor's friend Jed and a Vice President of the company. As tall as Connor he had the kind of loose, rangy build that always made her think of a cowboy. He had a cleft in his chin deep enough to stand an envelope in, an easy and engaging grin and wore a tux as comfortably as he would a pair of jeans.

According to the grapevine, if any of the secretaries couldn't have Connor O'Donnell himself, they'd have taken Jed in a heartbeat and not considered him second best. They all thought he was a sweetheart, a real gentleman but there were those in the upper echelons who had faced him across a conference room table who would have begged to differ. They referred to him as 'the Gunfighter' and swore there was no softness in the brown eyes the secretaries referred to as dreamy.

The other man was so fair, so blond, so tall and so broad in the chest and shoulders he reminded Cherry of a Viking warrior. He had dark green eyes in a handsome square Nordic face. That would be Erik. Another VP. Erik took after his Viking ancestors – he was always jetting off somewhere. From what she heard he had an instinct for where to find the next new investment, the next new location for an OI enterprise. Whatever he thought though, he kept to himself and the two men with him. To everyone else he was an enigma.

Somebody had told her once they'd seen Erik in the company gym, bench-pressing some ridiculous amount of weight, almost three times what she weighed according to her source. Which seemed unbelievable. Not even the most perfectly tailored tux could conceal the sheer breadth and depth of his chest and shoulders.

Three, count them, three, handsome men. All different. All gorgeous. All single.

The thought of even one of them touching her was enough to get her pussy wet and now one of them just had.

Her nipples had already contracted tightly beneath the warming strawberries, and now they tightened further. The juice of the strawberries trickled down the sides of Cherry's breasts and scented the air around her.

Bound to the table as she was what would happen from now on would be entirely up to them.

There were rumors around the company that the three were virtually inseparable, sharing everything — but weren't gay or bi. No one knew just how much of everything they shared, though. Cherry couldn't help but wonder. For herself, there was a touch of thrill, a little anticipation and a small trickle of fear at what she'd done and might be about to do. Tied by the soft but strong velvet, she couldn't move, so she was at their mercy whether they knew it or not.

She watched, her breath coming short as Connor picked up a strawberry from those scattered around her and brushed the firm rough fruit through the chocolate trickling down her ribs, then put it in his mouth and bit into the juicy piece of fruit. Her pussy tightened.

It was definitely decadent, erotic, even mildly debauched, Connor thought, as he picked up another strawberry and stroked it slowly through the warm chocolate dripping down her ribs just below her breasts, her glistening cherry lips parting again as she watched him from beneath long dark lashes.

Those big blue eyes turned toward him, and she shivered a little when he scraped the berry over her skin. She was sensitive. Ticklish.

Another bolt of heat went through him.

Even better.

Deliberately, he put the strawberry in his mouth, bit into the juicy fruit, her glistening cherry lips parting again as she watched him from her lashes. It was very good chocolate, the strawberry at its prime. Deliberately, he picked up a small crème puff, dipped it into the pool of honey between her full creamy breasts and popped it into his mouth.

Both Jed and Erik joined him, taking their time.

With an effort, Cherry kept from licking her own lips in return, her own juices flowing as she watched him, them.

Each touch, each slide of fruit across her skin, drove her increasingly crazy. Heat pooled in her belly, her nipples and pussy ached and her inner muscles worked with each dip and scrape. It was maddening, especially since she didn't dare move or Patrick's creations would crack or shift. Not that she could move much anyway, not the way she'd been bound.

Her torso and head were supported above the table by a narrow platform mostly concealed by her body but her arms and legs had been secured below her. In that position she couldn't move much at all.

All she could do was suffer the sweet delicious torment.

Curious, Jed dipped a strawberry in the pool of honey in her concave stomach. He watched her eyes widen as he swirled it around the cup of her navel. Scraping the fruit across her body was deliciously sensual. It was incredibly erotic to bite into it as her gaze followed the motion. He and Conn watched as Erik took another piece of pineapple, slipping it up the rounded swell of the side of her breast to gather the melting chocolate dripping there. Erik sucked the chocolate from it before sliding it across her skin again.

Her breath caught audibly, and she quivered.

That alone had him going hard.

His movements measured, Connor picked up a small cream puff, dipping it into the small pool of honey between her full creamy breasts to drag it over a lush curve, her eyes widening a little as he bit into the cream puff, the cream oozing out a little. He licked the little squirt of cream from his lips slowly.

Beneath his tuxedo slacks his cock was rigid, twitching against the fabric.

He loved it, loved this, loved all of it.

Around the room the other guests, oblivious to the sensual and erotic feast going on in front of them, dipped their own fruit or cakes into the different types of chocolate pooled around the chocolate statues or drank the fruit out of the glasses of champagne. That just added to the excitement of it.

One or two of the guests had snapped off pieces of the chocolate statues, one of the men daringly leaned across the small table to bite of the nipple of one.

Jed wandered over to head table in search of one of the fruit-filled glasses of champagne. His mouth went suddenly dry, and he took a swallow, his shaft as hard as iron.

Staring at the table, a small smile on his face, he called softly. "Hey, Conn. We have party favors."

Curious, Connor wandered over to join him.

Discreetly wrapped at each place setting of the main table was a bottle of fruit-flavored lubricant. A different one for each of them. And small squeeze bottles of honey.

He glanced over at lovely Cherry on the table, watching her blue eyes sparkle in the spotlights as Erik dipped a finger into the chocolate running down her body and licked it. She seemed to glow in contrast to the darkness around her, the narrow beams of pinpoint spots turning her hair to sparkling spun gold, the pale skin of those ripe, honey-covered breasts to lush ivory.

Her pretty lips were parted, her full white breasts, in sharp contrast to the dark chocolate, were rising and falling with her quickening breath.

Jed was right, she appeared to be enjoying this.

Discreetly, he slipped a hand into his pocket and adjusted his now throbbing cock.

A volunteer.

Help yourself to whatever you see, Patrick had said. *Enjoy your dessert.*

Connor looked at the party favors.

His body went even tighter, if that was possible.

He could take a hint.

Facing the crowd, Connor clapped his hands.

"Thank you, ladies and gentlemen," he said, "for coming. I hope you enjoyed your evening. Limousines await you below to take you safely home."

He wanted to enjoy the rest of his dessert in private…with his two best friends.

Chapter Three

For most of his life Connor had been searching for a woman like the one on the table, someone daring enough to do something like this. Now to his astonishment and delight he had her served up to him on a platter, as dessert. Looking down at the luscious honey, chocolate and sugar-covered body in front of him, her hands and legs bound to the table, her breasts lifted, and her shapely legs spread for his delectation, for once in his life Connor couldn't make a decision.

He simply didn't know where to start. Or how far would she let them go.

As it happened, this was a particular fantasy of theirs, his, Jed's, and Erik's. The three of them had talked often of all of them making love to one woman at the same time, sharing her between them, driving her crazy with pleasure, taking her to places she hadn't dreamed of going and taking their own pleasure with her in all the ways they wanted. A sex slave of sorts. Eating and being eaten. Doing her over and over again.

They had discussed it many times over beers and/or whiskey, in clubs or over a campfire, with plans made, ideas floated, positions debated.

Until now though, they hadn't had the opportunity or a partner willing to take all three of them at once.

Now, it seemed, they had. Maybe.

Those blue eyes watched them as if waiting to see what they would do next.

Jed didn't seem to have the same problem. He bent to slowly run his tongue up the inside of one of her shapely legs, gathering up the threads of rich chocolate from her ankle to her knee to a shiver and soft moan from the woman on the table, but no objection. The muscles of her leg tightened and quivered as Jed worked his way up. Connor had a fair guess what a delicious torment it was for her.

"I've wanted to do that since I first saw her," Jed said, looking at him, grinning, shaking his head and licking the chocolate from his lips. "That's really good chocolate."

Connor's cock twitched in his slacks as he watched Jed stroking his tongue over her smooth white thigh and seeing the muscles in it jump.

She certainly wasn't protesting.

Experimentally, Connor tested her bonds. Tight enough to keep her still but the velvet would prevent her from being hurt if she strained against them. It was clear she couldn't move much.

There's an advantage to that, he thought, with a smile.

She was lovely, especially with all that honey-gold hair spread around her, the honey and sugar sparkling from her fine features, from her firm mouth. Looking at her ripe red mouth, he wondered, looking at the rest of her, what it would taste like.

Curiously, he lowered his mouth to hers, touched his tongue to her lips and tasted cherries.

It was delicious. She was delicious.

A soft sound escaped her.

Connor smiled.

Slowly, he licked and sucked every trace of the cherry glacé from her soft lips. He traced the seam between them with his tongue and they opened for him. Covering her mouth with his, he tasted her.

She trembled, and Connor went even deeper, exploring her with his tongue, tasting the depths of her mouth, a soft sound of pleasure purring deep in her throat as he did. To his pleasure her tongue swept around his.

If there had been a moment for Cherry to protest it disappeared the moment Connor lowered his mouth to hers. Then he licked lightly at her lips, sucking on one, then the other and then on her tongue, tasting of cherries, chocolate and champagne. That kiss was amazing. Delicious. Delirious. His mouth moved over hers, sucking on her lips, and then on her tongue. She had to be dreaming.

Cherry hadn't known what to make of it when he sent the rest of his guests away but then Jed's mouth was on her foot and his tongue speared between her toes to get the chocolate there. Cherry thought she'd go insane as Jed began to lick his way up her other leg, the sensation incredibly erotic as he licked closer and closer to her core.

Combined with the sensation of Jed licking his way up her leg, his mouth moving up past her knee, her brain locked. A sharp jolt of pleasure had shot through her from where his tongue touched close, and then Connor's mouth had been on hers.

A cream puff swept over the curve of one of her breasts to the hollow between them and then up the curve of the other breast. The mental image of Erik continuing to eat from her as Connor and Jed did the same in their own ways sent another rush of erotic excitement through her. Her pussy throbbed and ached.

She thought she'd go insane as Connor kissed her brainless while Jed licked his way up her other leg until he was so close, so close to her core. Her cleft was drenched, pulsing. Heat rushed through her.

Quivering under the multiple assaults, she pulled futilely at the restraints, trying to get her hands free to run them into Connor's hair to pull his mouth down harder against hers. Or, as a bolt of heat shot through her as Jed nipped at the inside of her thigh, to clutch at the tablecloth or something, anything, as her belly tightened and her pussy clenched, aching. The knowledge she couldn't move somehow increased her excitement.

Cherry nearly lost her mind, awash in sensation.

The slightly rough sensation of a strawberry pressed against her navel. Erik.

Watching as Conn and Jed had had their way with sweet Cherry, stretched out on the table as she was, Erik dipped a strawberry deep into her navel, swirling it around, watching her stomach contract as he did it and his cock had gone even harder.

This was the most incredibly sexy thing he'd ever seen or done in his life.

Idly, curiously, his body already tight just looking at her spread on the table in front of him, he had traced the line of melting chocolate over one mounded breast with his finger, spreading his hand out over her to find her full breast would fill it as few did and his shaft went rigid.

A part of him couldn't help but wonder just how far they could go with her. A dozen fantasies raced through his mind.

His finger stopped at the artfully carved strawberry rose at the crest of her breast before picking it up to pop in his mouth.

And froze.

Beneath the strawberry there was nothing but sweet Cherry, her areole pebbled, her nipple ruched and hard.

And perfect.

Erik's breath caught, reverently.

He was a breast man through and through, small, large, he didn't really care but for him larger was a little better. Large enough to fill his big hands was the best and Cherry's lush mounded breasts were clearly big enough. With a sigh of pleasure, he touched a finger to her tightening nipple, rubbing it lightly. She trembled, her nipple going harder at his touch.

Bound to the table with Connor's mouth plundering hers and Jed working his way up her shapely legs, there was nothing she could do to stop him, and she certainly didn't seem to be objecting to Connor and Jed. In fact, judging by the soft eager sounds she made and the way she trembled, she wasn't minding this at all.

And that nipple looked sweet and tasty.

Slowly, he lowered his mouth to it, brushing his lips across it as she quivered.

Erik savored the taste and feel of her in his mouth, sliding his tongue over the rigid little nub as she twitched, moaning softly, shivering.

With a soft groan of his own, he drew that delectable little nub into his mouth to slide his tongue around it and her areole. He sucked lightly on them and she moaned around Connor's mouth on hers, the muscles of her stomach going taut beneath the hand he laid on her belly.

The chocolate breastplate was in his way, though.

Suckling and pulling on her nipple with his mouth, Erik carefully pried the thing loose. It slid away with a soft sucking sound and then her breasts were free. Mostly. Erik was more than glad to help get rid of some of the last traces of the chocolate on them. He swept his tongue over her lush fullness, sucked and nibbled at the ripe curves of her.

She was absolutely delicious.

Cherry was delirious. There was the sharper sensation around her nipple as warmth, a mouth, teeth, closed around it. Pleasure speared through her from there as well. She didn't know what to feel most, the moist slide of Jed's tongue slowly lapping its way up the inside of her thigh toward her aching core, the soft pull of Erik's mouth on her breast or the light stroke of Connor's finger across the other breast as he kissed her.

And she kissed him back.

His mouth was wonderful, his tongue dancing with hers, making her blood heat and her heart pound. He possessed her mouth, ravaged it more and more wildly, sending more heat racing through her.

Every woman had fantasies and this, having multiple men making love to her had been one of her wildest. She'd never expected it to come true. Not in a million years. And not so spectacularly. Her brain went into meltdown. Heat and tension pooled deep in her belly, poured out through her limbs until it seemed as if every nerve in her body was alight, as if she were ablaze beneath her skin, on fire, electric and charged. Her nipples were tight and aching, her pussy throbbing, wet and longing to be filled.

A mouth was on her everywhere, it seemed, she was drowning in ecstasy.

Her body quivered under the multiple assaults.

It dawned on her that they did indeed share everything and now, to all appearances, they fully intended to share her. They already were.

Excitement and a little trepidation raced through her.

To be honest she had wondered and even fantasized about what it would be like to be with all three of them, to have all three of them fucking her. An almost electric heat flashed through her as she realized she might be about to find out.

She couldn't stop quivering, trembling, her senses nearly overwhelmed by them and what they were doing to her. It was unbelievable.

With a sigh of pleasure, Connor lifted his mouth from hers, looking down the length of Cherry's lovely and delectable body as she quivered, watching Erik as he sucked at one luscious breast, his big hand full of it, and Jed working his way up her other leg with his tongue. She had his, their, kind of body, lush and full in all the places he and they liked. Her breasts were perfect, rounded, firm, just the way they liked them.

It was incredible to watch as Jed and Erik played with her, better than he'd imagined, knowing they were all enjoying themselves.

Including Cherry. She was enraptured, eyes half-closed, her back bowed a little.

Secured to the table by the red velvet ties, her hands twisted and turned in the velvet bonds, but she had been tied well. Something about the sight of her wrists straining against the velvet as she trembled and quivered helplessly sent a shot of pure lust straight to his throbbing shaft.

As Jed made his way up the other smooth, taut ivory thigh, her hips lifted in entreaty, her muscles flexed as she moaned softly.

Connor's body tightened even more, watching, seeing her lift her hips and ask to be sucked, fucked or eaten. If that's what she wanted they'd be more than glad to give it to her.

He ran a finger over one ripe ivory mound and then cupped the fullness of her breast in his hand, squeezing lightly, relishing her soft skin, the firm feel of it. It was still sticky.

She quivered at his touch, her blue eyes fluttering, glazed with pleasure.

So responsive. But just how responsive was she? And how often? How far would she be willing to go, or let them go? So far, she hadn't objected to anything they'd done, in fact as far as Connor could tell from her soft cries and moans, she certainly seemed to be enjoying it as much as they were.

He caught Jed's eye, lifted an eyebrow in suggestion. He knew what Jed and Erik liked, as they knew what he liked.

Jed would love this.

This would be a test of how just how far she was willing to go, how far she was willing to let them go. He had a pretty good idea he, Jed, and Erik knew exactly how far they wanted to go.

All the way and every way.

Nodding at Connor's look, Jed grinned. He'd been chomping at the bit for chance at this. The taste of the thin stripes of chocolate on Cherry's silky white skin had simply added to the pleasure, but with Connor's encouragement Jed was in search of honey now, his palms gently parting her firm thighs as far as the velvet bonds would allow. It was more than enough for him, giving him one of his favorite views.

For a moment he simply admired her, the tight curls between her thighs, the blush of her cleft.

This was Jed's particular fantasy, having a woman bound and helpless while he pleasured her, while he ate and sucked at her. He loved eating pussy, loved the soft sounds women made as he did it, loved watching their muscles twitch in response to the tease of his tongue, loved making a woman come again and again. As he wanted to do to Cherry.

Delicately, he parted the plump rosy folds of her cleft with his thumbs and held her open to him.

The rich musk of her arousal as well as the scent of chocolate rose to his nostrils but there was also the sweet taste of honey as his lips brushed over her mound and just over her labia. Just a tease.

She quivered and gasped lightly. He smiled.

Taking a deep breath, he inhaled her aroma, and then settled his mouth over her pussy, his tongue sweeping between her labia to the cream he knew would be waiting there for him before driving his tongue deep between them to taste her thoroughly and completely. She moaned, writhing at the sudden invasion.

So sweet, even without the honey.

Steadily and with real pleasure he took a long taste of her, the muscles within her clenching as she creamed. So nice.

He lapped at her clit, then going as deep into her as his tongue would allow, spearing it into her, sucking at her, tasting honey and Cherry as he slid his hands beneath her ass to angle her better. Her inner muscles twitched and flexed each time he went deeper.

Her eyes shot open as his mouth closed on her clit to suck and then as his tongue dipped deeply between her pussy lips, dragging slowly between them to reach her cream and she moaned as her hands twisted and turned within the velvet bonds. Her body grew taut, her back arched as she tried to raise her hips to him, pumping them.

Once again, he slid his tongue inside her to lick, to suck the juices from her, and her pussy gave it to him.

"God, you're sweet, Cherry," he groaned, sliding his tongue up to sweep around her clit.

She whimpered at the delicate touch.

Jed knew how to drive a woman crazy. He was going to drive Cherry wild.

Heat burst into flame inside her. Pleasure pooled around her core as Jed licked and fucked her with his tongue. She couldn't have protested if she wanted to. Her breath shuddered in her chest as heat and tension gathered inside her. The nipple in Erik's mouth was as hard as pebble as he suckled on her, too, nipped her, each pull of his mouth sending a bolt of electricity shooting through her to her core to join the heat stirred by Jed as he ate her thoroughly and enthusiastically, sucking hard at her pussy, at her clit.

Fingers toyed lightly with her other nipple, rolling and tugging on it.

She opened her eyes again and looked up, her vision hazed by the pleasure swelling within her.

Watching her, a small smile of satisfaction on his face, Connor O'Donnell played with her other breast, her other nipple, his fingers a sweet torment, his blue eyes intent as Jed and Erik drove her slowly insane. Knowing he watched made the pleasure more intense, more maddening.

Ecstasy built inside her, her pussy aching, flooding as Jed's mouth licked, lapped and sucked at her. Her clit swelled at each flick of his tongue against it. Pulsing, electric heat shot through her in flashes with each twitch of Connor's fingers on one breast, each scrape of Erik's teeth on the other, racing through her all the way down to her toes.

Her muscles tightened, and she quivered wildly, trapped by the velvet bonds, her back arching as she writhed, her eyelids fluttering.

All thought disappeared in the sensation as Jed's tongue slid up to lick, lap, and suck at her clit, at first lightly, then teasing and tormenting it. Each sweep and flick of it drove her up, higher and higher still, his tongue relentless as she moaned, nearly weeping with the desire to come, with the heat filling her but not taking her over the edge.

Connor watched as Cherry's blue eyes went wide, as they went blind, her system overcome by multiple sources of stimulation. He had no doubt Jed was enjoying himself, Jed's eyes were closed as he listened to Cherry's moans, his hands on her white thighs were pushing them further apart. Or that Erik was, who finally had breasts worthy of his big hands. One of which was currently closed tightly around one of her breasts, his teeth locked on her tightly ruched nipple.

Leaning down by her ear, Connor whispered, "Tonight, you're ours, ours to play with. Come for us, Cherry."

Jed suckled hard on her clit.

It was as if Connor's deep voice triggered the explosion inside her. Heat scorched through her and her orgasm erupted through her, a rocket of pleasure that shot through her, bursting outward from her core and skyrocketing through her body, seeming to take off the top of her head. She came with a sharp cry, her body vibrating wildly, helplessly. She shivered and shook as it burned through her, leaving her limp and trembling in its wake.

Dazed, Cherry looked up at Connor, into his gleaming blue eyes and something inside her quivered in anticipation at the look in them. At the heat and desire in them.

It was exactly as Connor had imagined and better.

Watching her come was absolutely incredible, color flooding beneath her fair skin as her body arched, trapped by the velvet ties, her hands opening and closing as ecstasy took her.

It was incredibly beautiful and erotic to listen to as she moaned and pleaded, her hips pumping, begging to be taken.

Taking one hard nipple in his hand, he twisted it lightly and she moaned, shuddering, as he slid his other hand into his pocket to slide it over his rigid cock. He was incredibly hard, throbbing.

He grinned. Her cry of pleasure and that moan were good signs, too. He liked women to be vocal, he wanted to hear a woman's pleasure, to know he had driven them so wild. Perfect.

Kissing her temple as she trembled in the aftermath of her orgasm, he whispered softly in her ear, "You're going to scream a lot tonight."

Quivering, she gasped, those soft lips parting once again.

With a lick to her nipple, Erik straightened. "She is a sweet piece."

"Let's see how many times she can come," Connor said.

"Wait," she said, her blue eyes widening, "I can't…"

Connor ignored her, glancing at Jed and Erik. If she had really meant it, if there had been real fear in her voice, if she had struggled, he would have. But she hadn't.

As if she hadn't spoken Jed said, in response, "She's at the right height, Erik, and she tastes incredible. It's like sucking the cream from inside a donut."

With a smile, Connor watched her stomach tighten in reaction. No, she definitely wasn't frightened. She was turned on, hot.

All of them were hard but having the opportunity to play like this didn't come often. Especially with a new toy and one as nice as this one, as vocal and as sweet as Cherry.

When I finally do come, though, I'm going to explode, Connor thought, stroking his aching cock beneath the tuxedo slacks, watching as she trembled in anticipation as Erik settled in between those white thighs.

It was beautiful to watch.

She still had too much honey and chocolate on her though and Connor wanted to play with those full, lush breasts, to squeeze and suck on them until her nipples were hard and so sensitive she would moan each time he touched them.

There were still some bottles of champagne left.

Connor's words sent a jolt of fresh heat through her. Cherry looked at him first and then Jed and Erik as their faces lit up.

Stunned, she watched as Erik leaned between her thighs and lowered his mouth to her still throbbing core. His tongue swept between her lower lips, tasting her deeply, lapping at her as Jed had, his thick tongue penetrating her repeatedly. Involuntarily she shuddered as a new burst of heat rushed through her.

Her eyes closed in ecstasy as Erik ate her eagerly, a soft moan she couldn't quell building in her throat as he fucked her with his tongue, sucking at her clit, her pussy, to draw her juices out of her, his tongue diving in to lick them out. Her pussy flooded to give it to him, pulsing and throbbing. Increasingly, she wanted something more inside her, something else, to have the aching void within her filled.

A cork popped.

Cherry shrieked as cold champagne drenched her overheated skin, breasts and belly, running between her thighs where Erik's tongue worked on her so enthusiastically. He sucked and licked it up as it ran between the delicate folds of her cleft, driving her crazy. Her muscles tightened as he pierced her with his tongue again, then ran it up to her clit, flicked it to lick up the champagne, before he drove his tongue into her pussy again.

Warm hands closed around and cupped her now cold breasts, squeezing them, massaging them, rolling the nipples between the fingers. It was incredible, marvelous, little electric sparks danced through her. Cherry loved having her breasts played with. One boyfriend had sworn he could make her come just from playing with and sucking on them.

Cherry had never been sure whether he wasn't right.

Dazed, she opened her eyes to see Connor's gaze locked on her breasts, his hands closed around them so tightly they swelled and she moaned — not in pain but in pleasure — as his mouth found a nipple. He sucked and suckled hard on her tender tip, bolts of pleasure spearing to her core.

Jed dipped his tongue into the pool of champagne in her navel and licked it up, his tongue spearing down into the cup and Cherry shivered at the touch as he sucked the last of the sparkling wine from it before making his way up her body to have his turn at her other breast.

The tease of Erik's tongue at her clit, along with the deep sweeping licks of it through her lower lips, drove her up, drove her higher. Jed's mouth closed around her other breast, both he and Connor suckling hard. Heat shot through her wildly. Erik's mouth slid up to her clit, sliding his tongue against it, deep sweeps of it across her sensitive nub, spearing against it, flicking it. Pleasure exploded. Crying out, she bucked hard as another orgasm punched through her, ecstasy rushing through her in a flood, heat pouring through her limbs in its wake. She shivered and shook with it, her skin on fire as it burned through her, scorching her.

His blue eyes hot, Connor looked at her and said with a smile of satisfaction, "Now we know she's multi-orgasmic. That's two. What say we go for three?"

She quivered at his words, she was limp, every muscle twitching, when someone held a bottle of champagne to her lips. She looked up to find Jed standing there holding the bottle, his brown eyes sympathetic but hot. She looked at him gratefully, drank thirstily and far too fast. On an empty stomach she knew the champagne would hit her like a ton of bricks, but she might need it.

While Cherry hadn't known what to expect, it hadn't been this, her wildest fantasy.

She might have dreamed of it, but she had never expected it to come true.

Every muscle shivered with pleasure, with need and desire.

She had agreed to put herself here though and now she could only surrender to it. There was no help for it, she was bound and helpless. And it was incredible. She had never been so turned on, so hot, in her entire life, much less had multiple orgasms.

There were three, count them, three, gorgeous men touching her, pleasuring her.

She smiled a little as Jed's mouth covered hers, his tongue licking at her lower lip, before sucking on it lightly. She opened her mouth to him and his tongue went deep, as someone massaged her breasts again and Connor's hand cupped her mound.

Jed tasted of the champagne and her own musk. His mouth was firm, but not too hard, as it moved over hers.

A groan escaped her as a finger speared up into her depths. Involuntarily her hips rose as much as she could lift them in that position.

God, she needed to be filled, to be fucked.

Connor lowered his mouth to Cherry's clit, touching just the tip of his tongue to it, his finger stroking within her as he searched for just the right spot inside. Her body clenched around his finger as Connor found what he had been looking for and stroked, his finger sliding over her g-spot.

"Dear God, she's so tight, so wet and so hot," he said as her slick internal muscles closed around his finger, "so sweet."

It was astonishing, the heat of her nearly scorching.

A soft moan whispered out of her as he stroked, and Erik returned to her breasts, devouring first one then the other, sucking and suckling hard on her until her nipples were rigid and distended, his hands closing around them, squeezing and kneading, his fingers pressed into the smooth, soft white flesh.

Cherry arched her back to give him more.

"Look at them, Conn," Erik said, his voice reverent, his hands filled with her bountiful tits, closed around them so they rose and mounded.

They were beautiful, that was certain, Connor had loved sucking on them, they were so ripe.

Sliding another finger into her Connor licked lightly at her clit until she moaned, her hips pumping as her inner muscles closed tightly, flexing around his fingers. Using her own juices as lubrication he brushed his thumb over the tight little entrance to her anus, pressing lightly. She trembled, hips lifting again. He pressed harder and her hips bucked.

He loved making love to women, but he had his own private fantasy that not all women enjoyed, one Jed and Erik shared.

Her head tossed as she fought the pleasure rising within her, her eyelids fluttering.

Promising.

Deliberately he swirled her clit with his tongue as he stroked her within and without, pressing his thumb against her anus lightly and listened to the wail building in her throat. He drew her swollen clit gently into his mouth and suckled softly but with steadily increasing force on it, listening as that wail built higher.

To his delight Connor watched Cherry arch as she poured into his hand, her body as tight as a bow as she cried out her pleasure once more. Her body trembled wildly as he sucked on her until she sobbed and then he released her.

Still bound to the table, she went limp, too weak to move, her head lolling, her hair sprayed over the table and around her lovely face.

There was no doubt in his mind now that pretty Cherry was multi-orgasmic and would keep coming until they stopped toying with her. Which could be a long time.

He looked at Jed and Erik, Jed with his hand in his pocket, stroking his cock beneath the fabric. Erik's erection pressed hard against his slacks.

As long as she was willing it looked to him as if they were keeping her.

Delirious, ecstasy washing through her, Cherry nearly wept as another orgasm swept through her. Her pussy ached. It felt empty. It needed more, needed to be filled. Each motion of Connor's mouth and tongue on her throbbing, aching clit had sent bursts of electricity through her body. The fingers inside her had driven an entirely new pleasure, deeper, far more intense. It was as if a dam had burst inside her. The flood that dam released had driven the cry out of her as it roared through her, her body bucking uncontrollably, instinctively trying to spread her legs for them despite being bound as every muscle in her body went taut.

She was utterly spent, wrung out, her muscles twitching. And they still hadn't fucked her, they had only toyed with her, teased and tormented her.

Cherry was only half aware when they untied her from the table, until Connor and Jed helped her to her feet, her knees shaking. Then Erik bound her wrists behind her with the velvet ties that had secured her to the table.

If she wanted to protest, now was the time.

Looking into Connor's blue eyes she saw them go hot as his hand slid between her thighs, cupping her mound, a fraction away from her throbbing, aching empty pussy.

"We're hardly through with you," Connor whispered in her ear, his lips brushing lightly over it, making her shiver. "We want you, all three of us. We've got the whole weekend ahead of us. We can make your wildest fantasies come true, Cherry. It's up to you."

She wasn't certain what they had in mind. A part of her worried but another part — her drenched, aching and empty pussy — wondered if she'd finally get to see them naked and whether they would fuck her or not. Right at the moment they could have bent her over the table and fucked her blind. All of them.

Individually, or each and all of them. She wouldn't have protested. She needed to be fucked, to be taken.

Looking at them, at the three of them, she could see they all had rigid erections tenting the material of their tuxedo pants.

Dear god but she wanted a cock inside her. One of their cocks.

No, she wasn't ready for it to be over yet either.

Taking a breath, she nodded.

She was committed now. She was their willing captive.

Chapter Four

With no one in the building to see they escorted the bound and naked Cherry up to the executive suite on the topmost floor of the building — to the living suite above Connor's office, accessed by private elevator and intended for those nights when Connor worked late, or too late to return home. It was the closest thing he had to home, now.

It was impossible for any of them, it seemed, to keep their hands off her lush and naked body, all three of them stroking and touching her breasts, her stomach, her tight, nicely rounded ass as they rode up in the elevator. Jed gave Connor a look, then slid his fingers along her rump, along her sex, his fingers slipping through the wetness there, giving her a quick finger fuck to hear her gasp. All three of them had grabbed bottles of champagne, drinking directly from the bottles, holding them for Cherry, the champagne spilling down over her breasts, over her body. All three of them sucked or licked it off.

The bedroom of the suite gave them plenty of space in which to play.

"All right, gentlemen, let's roll up our sleeves and get to work," Connor declared, smiling as they deposited Cherry on her knees in the middle of the king-sized bed, with her knees spread for balance…and the view of her pretty pussy.

Connor looked at her sitting there so prettily, so neatly, on the bed, her back so straight, her hands bound behind her so her gorgeous breasts pushed forward, the mound of curls and her sex clear and available to them.

Her golden hair tumbled wildly over her shoulders, her blue eyes were huge in a slightly heart-shaped face and her mouth was swollen from kisses. Her body was gorgeous, plentifully curved in all the right places, her full breasts heavy, lush and yet the hardened peaks of them still pointed upward.

Shaking his head, unbuttoning his cuffs, he could only admire her.

"God, you're beautiful," he said reverently, his cock aching to fuck her just from looking at her.

She was. It was amazing to see her there, naked, with the three of them standing around her.

Connor got no argument from either Jed or Erik, who were both eyeing her as well, their appreciation very evident.

The admiration in her eyes as she looked at them in return was just as obvious, her gaze wandering and lingering appreciatively over their bodies, very satisfying to three male egos.

Connor walked to the bed, unbuttoning his cuffs as he went, pleased when she raised herself unsteadily up on her knees to meet him.

For Cherry watching the three of them strip was like having her own private strip show as the white, pin-tucked tuxedo shirts came off, one after another.

She would have been hard put to say which she liked better — Connor's firmly muscled body, broad in the shoulders; Jed's long lean, narrow-hipped frame; or Erik's broad-chested, solidly muscled form. She swallowed hard as they quickly undressed, stripping out of their tuxedos, each hard, male body incredible in its own right.

It was clear all three worked out regularly, not just Erik, although the massive muscles in his chest, his arms, were testament to his dedication to keeping himself in shape.

Certainly, Connor and Jed had nothing to be ashamed of, there wasn't an ounce of excess body fat on either of them. They were just different body types. She didn't have favorites.

Then there were their cocks, especially Erik's and part of her grew wet in anticipation even as another quailed a little at the size of him, of it, thinking of him inside her, swelling inside her. He was a big man in more than one way but none of them were small. She was fairly certain she'd never taken anything as big as any of them into her at any time in her life.

It seemed likely she would tonight. Her head spun at the thought.

She knew if she asked they would let her go. They'd be disappointed, but they'd let her go. Looking at those hard, male bodies though, a rush of lust going through her, her own body still quivering from their attentions, she found she didn't want to leave. Not yet.

As they walked toward her all three looked at her as if she were a particularly tasty treat, something to be devoured… And after all, in a way she had been and still was. A shiver went through her, though, at that look in their eyes, the appreciation, the desire, the hunger in them. Her pussy flexed and tightened to see it.

Eyeing them, all of them drop-dead gorgeous, she said in answer to Connor, with a very real sigh of appreciation, "So are you."

They were.

Part of her wished her hands were free so she could run them over the strong muscles of Connor's chest, stroke over Jed's rippled abs, or run her fingers over Erik's massive pecs. She wanted to tangle her fingers in Connor's dark wavy hair, comb Jed's thick brown hair back, or Erik's silky blond.

With a smile, Connor walked toward her, took a handful of her hair, jerked her head back and proceeded to devour her mouth with enthusiasm as Jed and Erik settled to either side of her to stroke, play with and torment her body.

Their hands swarmed over her.

Cherry hadn't quite intended that when she'd done this but then Erik rammed his big thick fingers in her pussy while Jed suckled hard and enthusiastically at her breasts.

Heat exploded through her as they played with her.

Connor savaged her mouth, his mouth crushing hers, his tongue driving deeply into hers. She loved it, loved the fierceness of him, the passion. She loved the taste of him and his long, hard, naked body against hers.

"She's so tight," Erik said with a groan from behind her as his fingers pushed inside her.

His fingers were thicker than Connor's long ones and they stretched her delightfully as he finger-fucked her slowly and steadily. He plunged his fingers deep inside her, his big muscular arm wrapped around her back.

Moistening his thumb in her juices as Connor had, Erik rubbed it over the tightly puckered rosebud of her ass.

The pleasure it gave Cherry to feel his thumb there as he finger-fucked her at the same time astonished her. She didn't want him to stop any more than she wanted Jed to stop nipping and biting at her nipple — each nibble sent a sharp bolt of pleasure through her.

With each touch, her body jolted or quivered, urging them on to greater efforts.

Connor's hot mouth sent bursts of goose bumps over her and electricity dancing over her skin in concert to Erik's fingers inside her and Jed's mouth suckling hard at her breast, scraping his teeth over her other nipple. She was delirious, overwhelmed.

His fingers still inside her, Erik claimed her mouth next as Connor's lips wandered to her throat to the curve of it and her shoulder, sending a shower of goose bumps over her skin as his mouth settled there, sucking gently but steadily. Spurts of heat raced to her core, to her pussy. Connor's fingers slid down her belly to find her clit and play, teasing and tapping on it.

She was in sensory overload as heat poured through her, drowning her senses again.

As Connor had done, Erik broke the kiss off, his mouth tracing the curve of her jaw, then devouring her throat, biting and sucking as he went and she gasped, before settling in finally at the curve of her throat and shoulder, to suck hard, sending another wave of goose bumps over her skin.

Then it was Jed's turn to seduce her mouth, to play and suck as Connor slid down her body and off the bed, his hands cupping her ass to pull her hips forward so he could lick her clit.

Jed's mouth moved away from hers also, leaving a trail of fire behind as he savaged her throat in turn, nipping at her earlobe before his mouth settled above her collarbone. She quivered as he sucked and suckled at her throat. Each hard draw on the delicate, sensitive skin there sent a jolt of pleasure through her.

With an arm around her waist to keep her steady, Erik went to work once more on her breast, suckling, nibbling and biting as she quivered and trembled, his big hands squeezing her as he tugged on her nipple with his teeth, sending bolts of fire shooting through her.

Once more they made her blind and deaf to anything but what they did to her, Connor's mouth on her clit, Erik's on her breasts and Jed sucking on her throat. In all her life she had only ever dreamed of something like this, one of her naughtiest fantasies.

She loved it. It felt incredible to have all three men feasting on her like one of Patrick's desserts.

There was no part of her body that one or the other of them wasn't touching erotically in some way.

It was overwhelming, drowning her senses until she couldn't think, she could only feel. Electric heat seared from Connor's mouth on her clit all the way to the soles of her feet. Sharp jolts raced through her from Erik's mouth suckling and drawing on her breast. She arched her back to press her breasts against Erik's mouth, wanting him to suck harder, longing to have her hands free to curl around Jed's head to pull his mouth harder against her throat.

Her body ached, throbbed with need.

Ecstasy built, soared.

There was a growing pressure against her anus and she deliberately made herself relax to make the pressure ease. Instead something pushed inside her. She suddenly found herself penetrated and she moaned as Connor's thumb slid up into the narrow channel of her ass.

It didn't hurt precisely and in a way it was strangely exciting. Although she'd heard of anal sex, she'd never experienced it. It felt oddly and intimately invasive. There was a strange sense of fullness as he pressed. Each time her hips pumped in response to his mouth on her clit, they also drove her ass back against his thumb. That was a pleasure all its own.

Connor loved the fact that she was so vocal, so expressive that it wasn't hard to tell when she was coming. Her hips bucked in response to his thumb inside her ass, small cries escaping her. God, he needed to fuck her. What would her pussy be like? If the tightness around his fingers was any evidence, it would be incredible. He sucked savagely at the rigid little nub of her clit. He heard a high sound building in the back of her throat.

Now. He had to have her now.

Surging up her body, he drove into her, his rigid cock spearing deep inside her, toppling her to the bed.

His throbbing shaft slammed up into the depths of her, driving a cry of surprise and then a soft moan from her as he filled her. So tight, so sweetly, deliciously hot, she closed around him like a slick velvet fist, stroking him. He very nearly went blind as the pleasure of it shot through him. It was glorious. Brilliant. With each deep thrust he could feel the head of his cock hammering the top of her. He plowed her hard and deep, pulling out and then slamming back in, reveling in the astonishing tightness of her.

She felt amazing.

He pounded into her as her body closed around the thick length of his throbbing cock. Her pussy muscles clenched, pumping him. He swelled within her in response, iron hard inside her tight pussy. Her thighs opened to take him deeper.

"God, you are tight, so tight, so sweet," he groaned. It was damn near heaven.

He saw Jed and Erik watching as he fucked her, Jed stroking his own cock in anticipation.

What would Cherry's ass be like if her pussy was that sweetly tight? Connor groaned at the thought.

His cock throbbed, pulsed with the need for release, but he couldn't come yet, not yet, they had other plans, a fantasy they hadn't yet fulfilled.

They might have only one shot at it, he didn't want to lose it, as much as he wanted to keep fucking Cherry, fucking her sweet tightness.

"I want to come inside you," he groaned, "so bad."

She felt so damn good.

He bowed his head to touch his forehead to hers, to look into her dazzled blue eyes.

Cherry looked up into Connor's eyes, seeing the need in them, tension in every line of his body. Inside her his long thick shaft swelled, throbbing as he worked it inside her.

When he had slammed into her, his cock stretching her, going more deeply than anyone ever had before, it had stunned her. Suddenly she had been full, full of him, of Connor O'Donnell, filled with his cock. It was intense, marvelous, pleasure swelling inside her. Finally, finally someone was fucking her. Finally, he, Connor, was.

And then just as suddenly he was gone, pulling out of her body.

She moaned in frustration, in desperation and need as he pulled out of her, leaving her empty, still aching, still needing… If anything, it was worse for having had him inside her. The need to be filled…

Just as suddenly, she was.

A pair of hands closed over her hips, dragged them over the end of the bed.

Erik yanked her hips around and flipped her over onto her belly easily, as if she were nothing, before ramming the broad head of his thick cock deep into her pussy. She groaned as her body stretched to accommodate him, but there was only pleasure, no pain, as she took him. At the sound of her moan though he went more slowly now that he had penetrated her, working his hips a little to push inside her a bit at a time.

Caught off guard she had no chance to protest and then she didn't want to as his thick cock stroked inside her, the sweet friction of his swollen member driving deep inside setting her on fire.

Erik stretched her even more than Connor had as he drove into her, making her moan as he filled her inch by thick inch, burying himself in her all the way to the hilt. She moaned softly, letting out a sigh of relief and satisfaction.

It felt so good to have him fucking her, to have one of them fucking her.

Through the tumble of her hair she could see both Connor and Jed watching as Erik took her. With a smile, Connor reached out to tuck her hair behind her ear.

Her pussy clenched tightly around Erik's thick cock at the sight of them and Erik groaned.

"Fuck, Cherry," Erik said, his deep voice rumbling through her as he pushed into her once again, "you are so tight, so fucking sweet."

He pulled her up onto her knees, her cheek pressed into the blankets as he drove into her. Now with his hands locked on her shoulders, he pulled her up so he could go deeper, her back arching to take each deep thrust he drove into her.

When she opened her eyes, Jed knelt in front of her, fisting his cock, stroking it as he watched Erik filling her, Erik's hands on her shoulders holding her in place as Connor watched his friends fuck her, his blue eyes brilliant. Looking at her, Jed brushed the head of his twitching cock across her lips, a drop of pre-cum at the slit. It was a request, clearly.

Cherry looked up into his eyes, seeing the desire there.

She'd never done that to anyone's satisfaction before. The few times she had tried her boyfriend of the time had been too impatient and nearly choked her.

It was Jed, though. She was getting a sense of him, of the kind of person he was. And he had asked, in a way. He hadn't just done it. With her hands tied, she couldn't have stopped him.

All she could do was try. And she'd agreed to do this. He wasn't pushing it, forcing it, he was asking.

Tentatively, Cherry licked the salty taste of him from her lips and looked at him.

Jed shivered to watch her tongue sweep across her mouth to lick his cum from it. He desperately wanted those pretty lips wrapped warm and wet around his aching cock, he had dreamed about it from those first moments at the party. Cherry's blue eyes looked up at him, slightly unfocused, a little hesitant. He couldn't, wouldn't force her but God, he wanted her to do it, to suck him.

Watching him closely, she extended her tongue and touched it to his cock. His body tightened, his shaft twitching as heat shot through him. Opening her mouth, she took the crown of his shaft into it tentatively, running her tongue experimentally around the glans as she did. Jed's breath caught as that warm soft tongue swept across him and he shuddered with pleasure. Her mouth was wonderful, hot and wet.

To his astonishment though, it was pretty obvious she hadn't done this before.

He, they, would be more than glad to teach sweet Cherry the finer points of sucking cock.

Starting now.

"I won't hurt you," he said, quietly, watching as Erik thrust into her, seeing Erik's cock disappearing into sweet Cherry's pussy, Erik's hands tight on her hips.

Gathering handfuls of her hair, Jed rocked into her mouth carefully as Erik threw his head back at the pleasure her tight pussy around him gave him. Watching that gave Jed another jolt. His body tightened with the sensation of her hot wet mouth on him as he watched Erik fuck her, timing his own movements to Erik's.

"Suck on it, Cherry," he said and she did, her mouth wonderful around his throbbing shaft. "Yes. God, yes."

Carefully, he fucked that sweet hot mouth, watching her lips slide up and down his cock, taking himself slowly deeper with each thrust, letting her get adjusted to the size and length of him as he thrust deeper into her throat.

With luck, she would take them all, eat them all, sometime while she was here but just in case he wanted her hot, tight, sweet pussy around him, too, as Conn and Erik had. He wanted to experience all of her. They had all night, hopefully maybe all weekend. He wanted to take her in so many ways but none of them knew how long she would stay, or how long she would let them play with her. He didn't want to lose the opportunity.

Her mouth though, was absolutely incredible.

"Sweet Cherry," Jed said, with a soft sigh of regret as he withdrew from her deliciously hot, wet mouth.

Plowing into Cherry's soft wet tightness steadily, it was an effort for Erik not to come, to hold himself back, she was so sweetly tight around him. They had other plans for her, but it was killing him to restrain himself.

Not for much longer but still…

How often would an opportunity to play like this come along? They had been looking a long time for a girl like this and it was even better that she wasn't a pro. You could pay a hooker for something like this, but it just wasn't the same.

He tightened his hands on Cherry's shoulders, her pussy tight around his shaft, her long lovely back flexing as he drove deep into her hot, wet cunt, Jed's hands in her hair as he fucked her mouth. That was a turn on, too.

With Cherry stretched on her hands and knees between them, there was room beneath her and Connor took advantage of it, sliding under her to devour her breasts with relish, first one and then the other. Muffled wet sounds of pleasure slipped around Jed's cock. It was one of the most beautiful things Erik had ever seen, all of them fucking sweet pretty Cherry, her golden hair spilling over her shoulders, something they had dreamed of but never really thought would happen.

It was something to watch Jed's cock slide in and out of her mouth, to see how much Jed enjoyed it on him.

Erik was so close to coming, watching that, her sweet tightness close around him, the muscles inside her tightening. As much as he wanted to pump his hot cum into her pussy, he couldn't, not yet…soon, though, but not yet.

Reluctantly, he withdrew from her delicious tight wetness, her muscles flexing around him.

As he did, she moaned in something very like frustration, her eyelids fluttering, her body tightening.

That was the point and the plan, although they wouldn't, couldn't tell her that, so she wouldn't anticipate what they were going to do. They wanted her to want, to need to be fucked so bad that she'd just let them take her, do with her as they pleased.

As Connor took his place, he helped lift and steady her as Jed slid underneath her, guiding her knee over Jed to straddle him as she had Connor himself earlier. The sight of Cherry sucking Jed's cock as Erik fucked her had sent a jolt of heat through Connor, especially watching the pleasure on their faces as she took them. Both of them. It was incredible.

But if they were lucky, if they were careful, she might take all three of them at the same time.

That was their dream, to have all three of them fucking one woman at once.

"I don't think she's done much oral sex, Conn," Jed said, "but her mouth is wonderful."

Connor looked at him, not terribly surprised. For all that she was going along with this, there was an innocence about her. There had been a ring of truth in Monaghan's voice when he'd said she wasn't a pro and so far Connor had seen no evidence of it. She wasn't bold, she didn't initiate anything. She had a naturalness, a sweetness to her. Damn but she was game, though.

Had this been a fantasy of hers, to be taken this way, having two or three men all devoted to pleasuring her at once…?

Connor looked first at Jed and then at Erik in question. He had no need to say it. Both nodded. They knew him well enough by now to make talking unnecessary most of the time.

They would have their fantasy but if this was Cherry's fantasy they would try to fulfill hers, too.

There was no reason why it couldn't be as good for her as it was for them.

Somehow her innocence made it all the more exciting though, as if they were initiating Cherry into their world, into a world where sex was adult play, a pleasure and an adventure. This would be a safe place for her and them to play out their wildest dreams and sexual fantasies.

That she had put herself in this position indicated that at least some part of her had wanted to break out, to take risks and Connor understood that. He shared that need.

So he, they, would make certain to initiate her carefully, even gently, as much as they could.

Just the thought, oddly, made him harder.

With that in mind Connor carefully helped guide her onto Jed's twitching cock, watching her blue eyes widen, her lips part in a gasp as Jed filled her. Seeing that, seeing the pleasure in her eyes with Jed inside her, knowing that by now her pussy must be aching, that she must be half mad with the need to be satisfied and her all unknowing of their true plans, had him as hard as a rock. Her eyelids fluttered with pleasure as Jed thrust up into her, his hands on her hips, working his shaft around inside her to hear her moan. Erik palmed her breasts, teased them, squeezing them and playing with them.

Connor offered her his cock.

Those blue eyes opened and looked at him. For a moment she seemed to consider it.

When Cherry opened her mouth and took his head into it Connor could have sworn he'd died and gone to heaven. Watching as her lips closed around his rigid shaft, that hot wetness cover him, sent a shot of heat through him, his balls tightening. It took every effort to keep himself from coming right then and there. It was amazing. This was their fantasy come true. Settling his hands in her hair, he let Jed set the pace as Jed thrust up into her tight pussy, her gorgeous breasts shifting with the motion.

As Connor watched, Erik wrapped one big hand around one of her breasts, tugging on the nipple and then holding it for Jed to suck as Jed fucked her slowly and deliberately, wallowing in her by the motion of his hips and hers.

Each upward thrust drove Cherry's warm wet mouth farther onto Connor's rigid cock.

Opening the drawer of the bedside table, Erik coated his fingers with lubricant and looked at Connor.

Looking down at Cherry's soft lips sliding down his shaft as his shifted his hips to drive it carefully into her mouth, Connor nearly erupted at the thought but he nodded at Erik.

It was time. If it wasn't soon, he knew he'd explode.

Connor watched as Erik slowly, carefully pressed his lubricated finger against Cherry's little brown rosette, against that tight little hole. Even when she squirmed, though, Erik didn't stop, pushing gently but relentlessly, the lubrication helping as he slipped a finger inside Cherry's sweet tight ass.

Cherry jerked, groaning as the sensation filled her, over and above Connor in her mouth and Jed fucking her pussy. When she tried to wiggle away from that intimate invasion, though, both Connor and Jed held her gently but firmly in place as Erik's thick finger inexorably pushed inside her ass.

She'd never been taken that way, hadn't even really considered it until Erik's finger pressed against her, then pushed inside her and while it was strange, it wasn't bad. She just felt a little full, a little uncomfortable.

While she'd heard of anal sex and wondered about it, she had never had the chance to try it.

Jed slipped a hand between their bodies to stroke her clit with his long, agile and talented fingers.

A whimper escaped her as he touched her sensitized nub.

Pressing deeper with each thrust of his finger, Erik stroked into her lightly, in and out, pumping it as he went. She groaned softly as he kept pushing until his finger was deep inside her. He worked it there, thrusting and twisting. Pleasure filled her as she became accustomed to his finger so deep inside her, to the unfamiliar fullness in her ass. When he withdrew it slowly she felt oddly empty, only to have him turn around and press it and another firmly against her tight little hole.

Both Connor and Jed's hands held her in place.

Resigned to it, to them, she surrendered control and didn't resist as Erik slowly inserted both lubricated fingers inside her tight passage, pushing them deep, forcing a groan from her as he pumped them into her.

So full. It hurt but it didn't. She was strangely and deliciously stretched in a way she had never been stretched before.

She moaned softly around Connor's cock thrusting into her mouth, too full, yet there was Jed's long shaft inside her pussy, his thumb rubbing her clit. Erik's fingers pierced her, fucking her ass with a steady rhythm, his other arm coming around her body to support her, curling a hand around her breast as much to hold her in place as for his own pleasure it seemed. Then Jed caught that nipple once again in his mouth and Cherry shuddered with both Erik's hands on her, his fingers in her and Jed's mouth suckling hard on her nipple.

Then all three of them were fucking her in some way, Cherry arching her back to allow Jed's fingers access to her clit. Her vision blurred again as all three men used her thoroughly, completely, all of them thrusting into her. As she adjusted to the fullness in her ass, it became easier and then incredibly pleasurable.

So much pleasure. She drowned in it. She had never imagined this. She trembled and shook as heat built and swelled in response to Jed's clever fingers teasing her clit, even as his cock stroked inside her, Connor's thrusting into her mouth. Her pussy tightened around Jed, around the long length of his twitching cock inside her.

Once more she hovered on the precipice, her body quivering in response, the muscles inside her flexing, heat pouring through her. She was so close. So close. She was going to come.

Connor and Jed withdrew.

A whimper of protest whispered from her. "No, please."

That was what Connor had been waiting for, had hoped for, that they had worked her up so much she wanted to be taken, needed to be taken, any way they wanted to take her.

He smiled.

It was time.

Connor looked at Cherry.

She looked deliciously wanton with her golden hair wild over her shoulders, her beautiful blue eyes heavy-lidded with desire and lust. Her mouth was rosy and loose, her breasts swollen, the ruched nipples hard and distended. All three of them had marked her. Love bites decorated her slender throat although she didn't yet know that.

Those slightly dazed blue eyes watched him as Jed and Erik continued to play with her, keeping her aroused and on the edge, her muscles twitching visibly in response to their fingers teasing her.

Having her watch him as he prepared himself made him that much harder.

This would be amazing.

Deliberately, he poured lubricant over his cock, stroking his shaft slow and hard as she watched, letting her wonder what he was going to do, letting her figure out what he wanted from her.

Anticipation raced through him at the thought of taking her this way.

He lubed himself thoroughly before stretching out on the bed half seated, his back against the head of the bed, his cock more than ready for her. It stood upright from its nest of curls, throbbing and twitching.

"Come to me, Cherry," he said.

For a moment, she looked at him almost nervously and then at Jed and Erik. She bit her lip. Curiosity warred with her nervousness. He looked at her steadily, letting her make up her own mind.

Cherry knew what Connor had wanted, what they would do. He was going to fuck her ass, something she'd heard about, wondered about and always wanted to try. She needed desperately to come. She couldn't think her pussy throbbed so much, her body was on fire with need. She ached inside. Still, as she looked back at Connor's long thick cock, she couldn't help but be apprehensive.

Her breath caught.

Jed said, softly, the look in his long-lashed brown eyes reassuring, "Look at me, Cherry."

Slowly she nodded, locking her eyes on his brown ones.

In for a penny, in for a pound, but she also knew, or thought she knew, that they wouldn't hurt her if they could help it. She hoped.

Then she nodded.

Jed and Erik steadied her as they guided her to kneel over Connor, her back to him, her knees to each side of his hips.

He squirted lubricant on her, pressed the bottle against her ass and squeezing it so it forced some inside her before he slowly pushed his thumb into her, working the lubricant around inside her. The cool lubricant was oddly soothing at first and then it warmed. A glorious heat spread outward from it so that all her attention focused on that tight channel within her…and what was to come.

Watching that pretty, rounded white ass settle toward his cock sent an incredible rush through Connor. Then the broad mushroom head of his shaft pressed at that tight entrance, pushed against it, into it. She moaned a little, as much in anticipation as apprehension, he thought. He hoped. And reached for the bottle of lubricant.

She moaned softly as the broad head of his cock pressed against her, pushing at her tight entrance.

"Relax, Cherry," Connor said, "breathe and it will get easier." She nodded.

Jed and Erik eased her back into Connor's arms so that her own weight slowly but steadily impaled her on his cock as he held her and thrust gently upward.

Each thrust forced a groan from her as the head of Connor's cock pressed against her, into her, past her entrance, stretching her.

"God, she's tight," he groaned, pushing the head of his cock into her farther still, pulling almost out a little before sliding back into her ass as she gave a low moan and shuddered. "It's so good. You're so good, Cherry. So sweet and so tight."

He pushed deeper.

Full, too full. The head of his cock was so big, he was so long and yet Erik was even bigger… Her mind went wild.

Stretching out between her legs where she half-lay, half-sat with Connor's cock slowly impaling her ass, Jed lowered his mouth to her clit as she watched helplessly. His agile tongue stroked slowly licking and lapping at her steadily. With obvious pleasure Erik bent his head to her breasts, Connor cupping them and raising them for Erik to suck, his hands clenched hard around them.

Spreading his long legs, Connor pushed Cherry's even further apart as she sank further down onto the long thick shaft sliding into her ass.

She moaned, quivering as Jed's talented mouth laved her slit from pussy to clit, sending a rush of heat through her despite the fullness in her ass, each tug of Erik's mouth on her breasts sending an almost electric jolt straight to her core.

It became oddly exciting to have Connor inside her there, his cock slowly filling her, stretching her in ways she had never been stretched, the fullness strange, driving a deep groan of satisfaction from her as he went deeper. Jed's talented mouth against her pussy and her clit had its effect, too, especially as Erik suckled and nibbled at her now-tender nipples. Pleasure overcame the discomfort and her pussy flooded as Jed slid two long fingers up inside it to find her g-spot and stroke.

She was full of Connor, so full…and he filled her more and more deeply…

His hips pumped gently, driving up into her, a little deeper each time.

Jed's mouth was on her clit, sucking at the swollen sensitive little nub, drawing it out to suckle on it. Desire, need, poured through her. A third finger joined the others inside her pussy and Jed pumped them deep into her, stroking hard as Erik devoured her breasts, sucking and biting at her nipples, his teeth nipping, sending little electric jolts through her.

Overwhelmed, heat poured through her and she moaned, need and want drowning her, she needed to come, needed to be taken more deeply, to be filled more. She had to come, needed to come. It was too much, she couldn't take it.

She wanted…

Connor struggled for control, fought for it, the tightness of her delicious but nearly unbearable. He wanted to come with an intensity that was nearly overpowering. Carefully, he thrust into her, going deeper with each push into that incredible tightness, the pleasure of it hazing his vision. Each motion was like being stroked. It was an effort for him not to simply slam into her, to drive his throbbing cock into that brilliant tightness. Carefully, he worked his cock and the lubricant into her.

She moaned, shivering, each movement, large and small, driving her further down onto his cock, nearly driving him insane with the pleasure of her tight ass around his shaft. He wanted to fill her so bad, he was about ready to explode. Carefully he lifted her a little with Erik's help, but not all the way, before lowering her once again onto his throbbing shaft. She sank even further onto him this time, his cock going deeper still. It took an effort of will not to thrust, to give her body time to adjust to him.

Another long, soft moan was forced out of her, nearly undoing him. She trembled as she sank further onto him.

"Please," she begged, on another groan. "Oh, dear god, Connor, please."

She trembled, shook, her muscles twitching with each motion of Jed's mouth on her clit, with each tug of Erik's mouth on her breasts.

Connor looked at the other two in pleased surprise. That was better than he, than any of them, could have hoped.

Needing no further instruction, Jed sucked hard on her clit. Connor knew the moment he started. Her back arched, legs spreading wide, her body quivering as the orgasm took her.

He grasped her shoulders and thrust upwards, not that he could have stopped himself at that moment. The minute the words were out of her mouth, his cock had swelled and his own need had obliterated any thought. Then all he could think of was how intense it was, how brilliant it was to pump into that tight sweet ass. To pump into her, his hips driving his shaft deep as he and Jed held her in place.

Each thrust drove a deep moan from her.

In one swift movement Jed surged up Cherry's body, driving his own shaft deep inside her pussy, ramming it hard and deeply into her, holding there for a moment, his arms rigid as his eyes closed, absorbing the pleasure as he wallowed in her.

Cherry cried out.

Then, his movements in rhythm to Connor's, they began to thrust.

The shock of Jed filling her, of his cock suddenly ramming up inside her as Connor fucked her ass, blinded her to anything else.

Completely unaware of it, a cry was driven out of her.

She was lost to anything but the pleasure inside her, pulsing and throbbing, battering her as she found herself so thoroughly filled by them. It built as they thrust, Connor and Jed both driving hard, their cocks huge inside her, stretching her, swelling even further within her, driving her to delirium with pleasure as they fucked her.

A cock rubbed lightly at her lips.

Erik.

He knelt beside her, them, his green eyes dark with desire, his engorged cock in his hand, the other hand braced on the headboard.

Like Jed and Connor, he was asking.

Nearly mindless with the incredible pleasure of Connor and Jed fucking her, their cocks driving up inside her, even so she looked at the thick broad mushroom head of him, his shaft huge, her pussy tightened around Jed despite the daunting size of Erik in front of her.

She had taken Jed and Connor, how could she deny Erik?

Opening her mouth, she took him in, his thick cock wider than either Connor's or Jed's. It was a stretch, definitely.

He groaned with pleasure, his hand locking in her hair as he rocked into her.

Something about that sound, about knowing she gave him that much pleasure, eased something inside her.

There was a wonderful abandon to having all three men fuck her at the same time. Every orifice of her body was filled with one of them. With her hands still bound behind her, she couldn't do anything to prevent them but there was no fear, just pleasure. They let her choose at each step of the way.

Connor swelled inside her, stretching her even further, his cock pulsing inside her even as she sensed Erik trying to rein in control, his body rigid, his hand tight in her hair. Jed shifted, his throbbing cock inside her finding the right spot within her, rubbing against it and against Connor's shaft buried deep in her ass.

She drowned in ecstasy once more as they fucked her, each one driving into her.

Cherry wailed, her orgasm exploding through her, finally, ecstatic as Connor drove his thick cock up into her ass, filling it and her completely, her body quivering as much with the pleasure of Jed pounding into her as with Connor plunging inside her. Ecstasy burst through her and she shuddered as it punched through her, her body bucking wildly.

Cherry's cry of ecstasy was nearly drowned by Erik's cock in her mouth but the sound was enough for all three of them as her body shuddered, the muscles inside and out of her tightening, clenching, as she trembled wildly beneath them.

It was more than Connor could stand. With a shout, he came, emptying into the brilliant tightness of her sweet ass.

His cock seemed to empty endlessly, spurt after spurt pulsing into her.

She quivered, moaning, as his hot cum jetted into her.

His shout, his body going tight as he pumped into her and Cherry's cry and quivers triggered both Erik and Jed to come.

Connor watched as Erik's hands locked around Cherry's head and he thrust deeply into her mouth as he, too, finally came, Erik's massive body jerking as he emptied into her soft wet mouth.

At first she squirmed, struggling a little but then, surrendering, she stopped fighting and simply took what Erik gave her, her throat working, swallowing quickly, grunting with each swallow.

It was absolutely incredible for Connor to watch Erik getting off. He groaned with the sheer pleasure of it as he emptied into her.

The sight of it, watching as she surrendered to him, to them, was the final straw for Jed, it seemed.

He gave a shout, his body going stiff.

Desperately Cherry tried to swallow Erik's thick salty cum as Jed drove hard up inside her, spurting his own hot cum deep inside her pussy as he slammed up inside her, his body going rigid. Another rush of pleasure raced through her while she struggled to swallow Erik's cum, Connor still emptying himself inside her ass.

It was amazing, astonishing, knowing that all three of them were coming inside her, sharing their pleasure with each other and with her. Her own orgasm seemed as if it would never end as they filled her with their hot cum, their heat gushing deep into her ass and pussy.

For a moment, they were all frozen, locked in position as they emptied into her, pleasure obvious on the faces of Jed and Erik. Both looked sated, nearly dazed and supremely satisfied.

A surprising rush went through Cherry to see it, to know she had done that, that she had satisfied not just one or two but three men at the same time.

With regret, she gave a little sigh as Jed and Erik's cocks slid out of her and then Connor's, leaving her oddly empty.

They all fell back, limp and exhausted.

Connor's fingers tugged at her wrists and suddenly her hands were free.

With relief, she rolled her shoulders as Connor and Jed sandwiched her gently between them, their arms curling around her to pull themselves closer, easing her down between them as Erik slid down between her legs to lay his head on her belly.

In wonder and pleasure Cherry ran the backs of her hands over Connor's and Jed's chests and then reached down to brush Erik's pale hair back with her fingertips. Her hands shook. She trembled with exhaustion, every muscle twitching as she licked her dry lips. She was dazed, her mind absolutely blown.

For a moment, except for her brushing her hands across Connor and Jed's chests, none of them moved.

Connor's lips brushed her ear, the motion sending a shiver through her.

"Are you all right?" he asked, softly.

"Ummm," she said, shakily, smiling, "Ask me in an hour, after I find out if I can still think."

It would take at least that long. She'd never been fucked so completely and thoroughly in her life.

A small incredulous laugh escaped her.

He chuckled, too, the vibration rumbling through her body at the same time she heard it.

Looking at him, at his strong handsome face, his blue eyes brilliant, the lines of tension she hadn't noticed until now falling away and her heart caught. That wouldn't do.

"Bathroom…"

Not surprisingly, Cherry found her knees wobbly.

After taking turns, they gave her a few moments of privacy.

One look in the mirror had her reaching for the soap to wash the makeup from her face, and a little water made the sugar in her hair soften so she could scrunch it. The soap had a slightly spicy scent to it that she liked. A glance at all the myriad dials and jets in the shower made her decide to settle just a quick and thorough cleaning with a cloth.

She stepped out of the bathroom to find them waiting.

With the heavy makeup removed to Connor Cherry looked like a sweet fresh-faced Midwestern girl, and suddenly he found himself looking forward to debauching that pretty farm girl.

Tomorrow. Tonight, they needed to sleep.

In one quick move he tossed her over his shoulder. She laughed.

"Put me down," she protested half-heartedly.

"No," he answered with a grin.

With her bottom available, both Jed and Erik each smacked one of those rounded ivory globes.

She yelped.

"Why do you keep doing that," Cherry said, not really complaining as she squirmed to try to get a look at them.

Connor just hefted her more firmly into place.

"Because we can, and because they're so nicely soft and rounded, just perfect for smacking," Jed answered, his eyes twinkling.

Then Connor tossed her into the middle of the bed, and Cherry found herself surrounded by firm male bodies.

Cherry looked at Jed and then at Erik with his head pillowed on her belly.

Then Connor snuggled up against her back with an arm over her waist and Jed stretched out beside her, his head against her shoulder, tucked a little beneath her chin. Idly she turned her head to brush her cheek over his thick brown hair.

Erik curled an arm around her free leg and settled in comfortably.

The gesture took her by surprise and made her heart twist a little. She reached down to touch his hair.

It felt wonderful.

She couldn't believe it. She was in Connor O'Donnell's private suite in bed with not just him but his two best friends. And they had just thoroughly fucked her. Every nerve in her body still hummed from it.

They had to be as tired as she was.

Not surprisingly, she fell asleep that way.

Chapter Five

A warm mouth fastened onto her breast, suckling lightly, delightfully, licking and teasing. Still half-asleep Cherry moaned softly with pleasure, her nipple a little tender from the attentions of the previous night but the gentle pulls on it sent heat spiraling sweetly through her. She curled her fingers into thick hair to draw that wonderfully soothing mouth a little tighter against her. She felt wonderfully and well used, her body aching in all the right places. Her nipples felt a little scraped but that soft warm mouth soothed them nicely. It had been a long time since she had been so satisfied. She couldn't remember coming so often or so deeply in her life.

Cherry opened her eyes to find Jed, his warm brown eyes closed and one arm around her waist to draw her closer, sucking contentedly at her breast.

The sight of it sent a rush of warmth through her.

Connor curled against her back, his leg tangled with one of hers. They were all three lying in a mesh of bodies. Erik's head was pillowed on one thigh. It was a lovely tangle.

She smiled.

Behind her, Connor stirred, his hard erection slipped between her thighs, rubbing against her dampening pussy, his hand on her hip as his own pumped drowsily and his cock slipped and slid through her juices.

"Good morning, Cherry," Connor said, against her ear.

His voice was soft and deep, making her shiver a little, especially as he pressed a kiss beneath her ear before he nibbled lightly at her earlobe.

"Good morning," she murmured back, sighing happily, still not quite awake, little waves of warmth moving through her from Jed's mouth suckling steadily on her breast and Connor's cock shifting between her thighs. Connor bumped his hips against her ass.

It was hardly the worst way to wake up.

Then it got better.

Movement rocked the mattress as Erik changed position.

Nudging her thighs further apart he spread her legs gently, his thick fingers playing surprisingly lightly with her clit. His dark green eyes focused on her face, watching her, watching Jed sucking at her breast. She knew he was aware of Connor, of what Connor was doing.

Heat flooded her sleepy mind.

Now, this was heaven.

Shifting her a little, Connor drew her back against him until she lay almost on top of him, one leg wrapped around hers to hold her open for Erik. Pleasure speared through her. Connor's hips rocked against her bottom so that his cock slid through the dampness between her thighs, especially with Jed's mouth on her nipple adding to the pleasure. Her pussy got wetter as Connor's cock slid across it, tantalizingly, especially as Erik teased her clit.

Heat gathered and pooled low in her belly.

To her astonishment and pleasure, she knew she was going to come again. With an effort, she tried to keep her hand loose in Jed's hair, reaching behind her with the other one for Connor as sensation poured through her, as pleasure buffeted her.

Connor felt Cherry trembling, her body quivering against his, her pussy warm and wet against his cock. Her hand closed over his hip, clinging to him as the storm of her orgasm shook her.

Something inside him tightened and warmed.

Waking up to Cherry in his arms, he had had an instant hard-on, but having her reach for him was a new sensation entirely.

It wasn't unusual by any long stretch of the imagination for him to wake up with morning wood, but with Cherry soft and warm against him, his dick between her thighs…?

Nothing in Connor's life had prepared him for this, for her. He had avoided that, until now.

He had never wanted a woman as bad as he had than when he awakened with Cherry against him.

As many women as he'd made love to or fucked over the years, he had slept with a rare few. But awakening with Cherry's lush and lovely little body curled into the curve of his had been sweet, sexy and irresistible. With her body against his, his cock was absolutely incredibly hard. He couldn't believe how hard he was.

He wanted her with an intensity that nearly overwhelmed him but he also relished the delicious sensation of his shaft sliding through the liquid warmth between her thighs.

There was something about his hard cock against her soft wet pussy, his flesh against her flesh that was just incredible.

With a little moan of need, though, she shifted her hips, angling them. Then he was inside her heat, her sweet tight moisture, her body quivering and closing around him as his cock pierced her. Connor groaned with the pleasure of it, of her heat closing around him. She was so tight, so incredibly hot and wet. As Jed suckled her breast and Erik played with her clit, the muscles inside her flexed deliciously around his cock. It was as if her pussy stroked him, making him harder.

Cherry writhed and trembled in his arms, soft cries and gasps escaping her as he and they, Jed and Erik, tormented her.

He loved it, loved every tremble, loved holding her as she quivered.

Gloriously, she erupted, her vaginal walls clenching around him, pumping him as her hips bucked, as they pumped, milking his cock until he exploded into her even as she shuddered and trembled in his arms.

It astonished him.

Connor pulled reluctantly out of her pussy, watching as Jed slid off the bed, reaching to draw Cherry's legs after him, to turn her over so that she was bent over the high mattress.

A different kind of excitement went through him, knowing what Jed was about to do. He hadn't had the opportunity to watch the previous night.

What Cherry did for one, she would have to do for the others.

A little startled, Cherry looked back over her shoulder at Jed as he parted the cheeks of her ass.

Remembering Connor taking Cherry up the ass the night before and sporting some impressive morning wood himself, Jed reached for the lubricant. Waking up to find her breast there in his face, he hadn't been able to resist sucking on it. Listening to her come, watching her pretty face still soft with sleep as Connor fucked her and Erik played with that plump little clit of hers, had reminded him of what he had missed the night before.

Wrapping his hand around his cock, Jed pumped himself harder. He wanted a piece of that, too, now that Connor had broken her in properly.

The height of the bed was perfect. Her shapely legs dangled, spread as she looked back at him.

Grabbing her hips, Jed watched her eyes as he pressed his cock against the tight little rosebud of her ass and thrust, pushing past the tight entrance. She threw her head back, her back arching. She groaned as the broad head of his cock pierced her, stretched her.

Jed slid his hands up the long lovely lines of her back, curling them over her shoulders to get a good grip.

Her sweet ass was so gloriously, unbelievably tight.

She moaned softly, shifting a little beneath him as he drove steadily into her until he was seated all the way inside her, buried to the hilt inside her tight ass.

It felt incredible. For a moment he held there, basking in that tightness around him, no matter how much his cock throbbed, no matter how much he wanted to pound into her, to erupt inside her, to fill her with his hot cum.

"Cherry?"

Quivering, she breathed, "Yes."

Slowly and deliberately, he plowed into that pretty white ass, going deep and hard, hips pumping against her as Connor and Erik watched, Erik stroking his own rigid cock even harder. Something about them watching seemed to make him harder. Cherry moaned, writhing beneath him, turning Jed as hard as iron, his cock pulsing inside that tight, tight sheath.

She was so snug, so sweetly tight he almost couldn't stand it, it was nearly more than he could bear.

She lifted that firm ass to him, asking for more.

It almost stunned him.

The sight of it only made him hotter.

"Oh, god," she cried out as he thrust deeper into her.

Her tight ass closing around him nearly overcame him but Jed wanted to enjoy fucking it, he wanted to savor her, so he worked every inch of his long shaft into her as she moaned softly, her hands clenched in the bed coverings.

He was losing control, his cock swelling inside that astonishing closeness. Her ass was so tight.

"God, Cherry, you feel incredible," he said, just before he exploded inside her, gushing, pumping into her warmth.

She cried out as his hot cum jetted inside her and filled her body.

With a shuddering sigh, Jed ran his hands down and up her long, graceful back as he collapsed over her for a moment, his shaft still buried inside her. He braced himself on one arm, brushing her hair carefully away from her face so he could see it, kissing her shoulder tenderly as he pulled out of her.

This was what they had wanted, their own private orgy, watching each other take their pleasure. He had thought once of hiring a professional but a professional wouldn't have been as good, they wouldn't have known for certain that she was really enjoying what they did.

It was clear that Cherry did. A dozen chances to protest had come and gone and she hadn't demurred once. Even more, though, was the way she moaned, the way she lifted her hips, or writhed beneath him.

No, a professional couldn't have matched Cherry. She was incredible.

He looked at Erik, shaking his head.

"Man," Jed said, "you have no idea."

A little dazed, Cherry felt Erik move behind her for his turn, Jed having prepared her, opened her a little for him. Despite Jed's preparation Erik's cock still seemed huge and thick against her ass as he parted her rear cheeks and pressed the crown of his shaft against her tight little hole.

She grunted as Erik's huge cock pressed at her tight entrance.

For a moment she almost protested and then the head of him pushed inside her spreading the tight sphincter of her ass. She couldn't speak as the pressure of it, the pain and pleasure of it, drove a deep groan from her as he drove into her and filled her.

He was so very big that a part of her shivered. He grasped her shoulders as Jed had, pushing steadily and seemingly relentlessly into her. The head of his cock seemed huge inside her.

Cherry wailed, whether in pleasure or pain she couldn't say. Thicker than either Connor or Jed, Erik stretched her ass nearly painfully despite the lube. Connor stroked her hair, the motion soothing and then all she could feel was Erik's thick cock driving deeper into her ass.

She gasped and groaned as he filled her slowly, steadily, relentlessly, trying not to struggle against it, against him, his thick shaft stretching her more and more as he went deeper inside her.

It was incredible, Erik thought. Nothing had ever felt this good, this tight. Watching Jed as he fucked Cherry's ass, watching Jed's face as he did it, Erik had lubed up for his turn.

It was better than he could have thought possible.

Cherry was astonishing, sweet, lovely, responsive and as willing as hell. How many women could you find like that? All he wanted to do was fuck her over and over again as they had been, every way they could take her for as long as they could take her, as long as she could take them. He loved her big breasts, the way they filled his hands and he got harder remembering her hot mouth around him as he fucked it. He had wanted a piece of that tight little ass, though, too.

Now he had it.

And she was gloriously, deliciously tight, writhing beneath him. He'd never fucked anything as tight as Cherry, she was almost painfully close around him.

Her back arched as he filled her, burying himself to the hilt in her, balls deep, holding there for a moment, his mind going blank from the pleasure of her so tight around him. Slowly he withdrew. Almost completely. Almost.

He ran the head of his cock around in her tight, tight ass as she shivered, a low moan whispering from her.

"God, you feel good," he groaned.

It was incredible. She was incredible.

She moaned deeply as he pumped his hips, the crown of his cock working inside her, going deeper.

Erik looked at Connor and Jed, both watching as he struggled for control. Another burst of excitement went through him. Carefully Erik slid deeply inside her again, her tightness maddening, delicious.

There was something else, though.

Wrapping his arms beneath her legs, in one smooth motion Erik bent and scooped Cherry up, her back against his chest. In that one motion she slid further down onto his pulsing shaft, driving a long shuddering moan from her as she was impaled more completely on him.

It was glorious, incredible.

Turning, Erik spread her legs for Connor as he pumped deep into her ass.

Cherry thought she'd lost her mind. She couldn't believe the power in Erik's massive arms as he picked her up. He lifted her as if she were nothing, his thick cock completely buried in her ass. She groaned, the sound forced out of her as the thickness of him filled her so utterly and completely.

Her eyes hazed as, to her astonishment, Connor took the offering that Erik had made of her, his own expression incredulous as Erik spread her for him.

Amazed, shaking his head, Connor reached out to brush his thumbs over her nipples as Erik hefted her a little and her weight drove her further down onto his thick cock. A low moan escaped her again as his shaft drove deeper.

Her vision seemed to waver with the intensity of it but she could see Connor's blue eyes go darker as he touched her.

That delicate touch sent heat spiraling through her.

Despite herself, she whimpered.

Still shaking his head, Connor lifted his head, his gaze going to hers as he slid two fingers deep into her pussy, driving another low groan from her as he stroked them into her. Her internal muscles tightened and Erik matched her groan. That brilliant blue gaze held hers as Connor slid to the edge of the bed, lowering his mouth to her clit to savor it, his fingers stroking inside her.

In all her life she had never even imagined this.

Connor's warm mouth and tongue moved over her clit, lapping at her as dreamily as a cat would a bowl of cream, his fingers stroking her as his gaze held hers until pleasure swamped her once more.

Stretched out on the bed behind Connor, Jed watched avidly, his brown eyes fixed on them, on her.

Lightly, Connor's tongue teased at her clit.

"Oh, god, I love your mouth on me," Cherry gasped, each stroke of his tongue sending torrents of bliss through her as Erik pumped into her ass, Connor's hands on her hips keeping them still so that each of Erik's thrusts went deep.

Erik swelled within her. She moaned as he stretched her even more.

As Connor teased at her clit control and thought disappeared, her hips bucking in response to each lick and swirl of his tongue. She whimpered, whined, she was so close, so close to coming.

"Please," she begged.

Connor drew her clit into his mouth, suckling hard on it.

A shriek tore out of her as she came, her body bucking wildly, Erik swelling within her, roaring his satisfaction as he came right behind her, his hot cum pumping into her, filling her ass as his arms locked tightly around her.

Legs trembling with the force of his orgasm, Erik dropped forward, Cherry beneath him, his cock buried deep inside her ass, pushing his gushing shaft deeper still, bracing himself on one forearm. He laid his forehead against her back, breathing hard but steadily, his other arm tight around her waist to hold her close and keep his weight from falling completely on her. For which she was grateful. She was absolutely certain that she couldn't move.

Jed nudged Erik, "Move, Erik or you'll squash her."

"I don't know if I can, Jed," Erik said, pressing a kiss against her temple, the gesture surprising her. "Cherry, that was incredible, better than I could have imagined."

Connor gathered her up in his arms, into his lap, looking down at her as he brushed the hair away from her face, kissing her gently.

"Are you all right?" he asked.

His concern gratified her, soothed her.

Especially once Jed took her hand to press a kiss into the palm of it.

"Erik's right, Cherry, you are incredible," he said.

That was satisfying, too, but she was limp, though, utterly wasted. She couldn't have moved even if she wanted to. Her muscles were still twitching wildly.

She was startled to find Connor gathering her up into his arms.

While he might not have been as broadly muscled as Erik, he still lifted her as if she were nothing. More, his arms closed around her in such a way that she had little choice except to wrap hers around his neck, her face buried against his throat. Beneath her lips his pulse beat strongly.

She felt oddly cherished. Her heart twisted more than a little.

As much as she wished otherwise though, she knew she probably imagined that his arms tightened around her when she pressed her mouth against that throbbing pulse, his life beating against her lips. She couldn't for the life of her figure out why she suddenly wanted to cry.

"We all definitely need a shower," Connor said, his voice sounding a little husky.

It was nothing more than the truth.

The air was filled with the scent of their musk, their cum and Cherry's pleasure and while no one seemed to mind, there were parts of her that were still sticky from more than just sex.

All of three of them seemed to be watching her carefully, though, as Connor set her on her feet, both he and Jed with an arm around her to support her.

She looked at them, at the concern in their eyes and smiled reassuringly.

"I'm fine, really," she said, as Connor put her down.

The shower was huge, with multiple showerheads and jets coming from almost everywhere it seemed. The three men hemmed her in and supported her as warm water sprayed soothingly against Cherry's overused and abused muscles. Her legs trembled and some of her muscles still twitched. It was a relief, too, to wash the last of the makeup away.

All three of men filled their hands with soap from the dispenser on the wall to lather her up, their hands gliding over her, gently massaging her sore muscles.

With a smile of real pleasure as her strength returned, she repaid the favor.

Shaking her head in wonder, smiling, she ran her hands over three gorgeous bodies, filling her hands with the slippery soap to run them over Connor's sculpted chest, his washboard stomach, stroking them over Jed's leanly muscled body, or running them across Erik's amazingly broad pecs.

With a long sigh, she said, suiting action to words, "You're all so beautiful. You're wonderful to touch. I can't get enough of you, you feel amazing."

Pulling her closer, his soapy hand gliding over her, Connor said, his blue eyes brilliant in the lights, "The feeling is mutual," emphasized the word 'feeling' by closing his hand around her breast.

She smiled at him.

Jed, too, had soaped his hands thoroughly and his long fingers were sliding over her, between her legs, playing a little, his brown eyes knowing, mischievous and teasing as he first rinsed his finger off before he slid it inside her, then two, working them inside her as if he cleaned a glass. Cleaning her. She moaned, the pleasure unexpected.

Taking one of the detachable and adjustable showerheads, Erik rinsed her off, playing the pulsing jets against the abused muscles of her shoulders. His arm around her, Connor held her close against him and Cherry let her head fall against the broad muscles of his chest, relishing his arm around her and the warm water beating at her strained muscles soothingly. Sighing with pleasure, she relaxed.

Connor pressed his mouth against her ear.

"You can stay if you like, Cherry," he said softly.

Lifting her head, Cherry looked up at him.

There was an intensity in his blue eyes that she hadn't seen in them before this. His hands had tightened on her.

Glancing over her shoulder, she looked at Jed and Erik.

Jed slid a hand over her ass, over her hip. He looked at Connor and Erik.

"We'd like you to stay at least a little longer, if you want."

Erik nodded.

"But we're not done playing with you," Connor said. "You know we'll fuck you again. Probably more than once."

A little thrill went through her at their words, at the idea. Despite everything they had already done, to her astonishment her pussy flexed and clenched, especially as she looked at all three men.

Jed stepped in closer, his hand sliding up from her hip to cup her breast.

She looked into his steady brown eyes.

Every inch of her skin seemed aware of Connor's long, strong body pressed against hers, at the tightness of his hands on her.

Water poured over them.

She looked at Erik. His green eyes looked evenly back, but she knew he waited for her answer.

With a half laugh at herself, knowing she wouldn't walk comfortably for a week at this rate, she considered it.

How often, though, would she get an opportunity like this, to have three gorgeous men fucking her and making love to her?

What did she have waiting for her back at her apartment but files to review?

Taking a breath, she looked at the three of them again and then looked up into Connor O'Donnell's brilliant blue eyes.

"Maybe I can convince you," he said, those eyes twinkling mischievously, reaching for one of the other spray heads and giving Erik and Jed a look.

With his gaze locked on hers as Erik played the soothing spray over her shoulders, Connor directed the pulsing spray over her breasts. Then down her belly.

All three of them were grinning like mischievous boys.

Cherry gave them all a wary look but she couldn't help shaking her head and smiling back.

She took a long slow breath though as Connor played the spray down her body as Jed slid his arm around her below her breasts to hold her in place, Connor letting the water dance over her mound and lower.

Taking his gaze from hers Connor angled the lightly pulsing jet of water against her clit.

Her body tightened and she clenched her teeth.

"That's not fair," she protested.

Connor grinned. "I'm a businessman, I don't play fair. Not if I want to make the deal. It's the art of the deal and I am the master of it."

Rolling her eyes at him, she fought a smile even as a wave of delight washed through her, both at their expressions and at the water tormenting her.

"Is that so?" she said, fighting laughter, her voice sounding a little tight even to her own ears as she fought the sweet tension rising within her.

Water beat in a steady rhythm down her back to pummel against her as Erik redirected the flow of his nozzle.

"It is." Angling the showerhead while Jed tightened his arm around her, Connor played it over her pussy and clit. "Stay with us, Cherry. We'll make it worth your while. We'll make all your wildest dreams come true."

She looked at the three of them. They already were.

Heat poured through her not just over her.

The water was relentless. It beat against her, driving up inside her. A different kind of heat built, this one inside her.

She moaned softly, giving them all a look.

"All right," she said, shifting, trying to escape the tormenting play of the water.

"We have to make sure you're thoroughly rinsed," Connor said, grinning, directing the pulsing spray against her clit, angling it slightly, and then her pussy.

"You know," she said, her voice sounding slightly strangled as the pounding sprays of water sent small bursts of ecstasy through her. "You're going to ruin me…"

A little startled, Connor looked at her. "Ruin how?"

"What other man is going to come close to even one of you three?"

Much less their inventiveness. The pulsating water drove her crazy.

It beat against her clit and the tight entrance to her ass, the rhythm maddening. Every muscle in her body tightened again as heat flooded her in more ways than one.

Jed looked at Connor.

"There's that," he conceded with a grin.

Connor wasn't sure that she wasn't going to ruin them. Where would they find another woman willing to allow three men to fuck her the way they were her? With as much as evident and vocal enjoyment?

Which was one of the reasons Connor wanted her to stay.

Those pretty blue eyes closed as the muscles in her belly that had eased tightened once again, soft moans escaping her as he and Erik directed the pounding water over her breasts, against the tight rosette of her ass, against her pussy and clit until she trembled and quivered. With a smile, Connor reached and turned the water pressure up, directing it against her clit, his arm around her, too, now, as much to hold her in place as to support her.

It amazed him to watch her coming apart as he teased her with it, a soft wail building in the back of her throat as he focused the pulsing spray on the small bud of her clit, Erik at the tight brown rosebud of her ass, grinning.

She quivered wildly as Connor forced the pounding, pulsing spray closer and closer to her, the water not allowing her clit to retreat, Erik angling his spray between her spread legs so that it beat against her pussy.

Her eyelids fluttered.

"Tell me what you want, Cherry," Connor said, pressing his lips against her ear.

She moaned. "Oh, please, Connor."

"We've got you, Cherry," Jed whispered.

She shattered in their arms as they watched, color flooding her skin, her body jolting and bucking.

Connor and Jed held her tightly as she came down from her orgasmic high, Jed kissing her temple affectionately.

Then the three of them even washed her hair, getting the last of the sugar out of the long strands.

All three helped dry her off. She laughed as they rubbed her down thoroughly before pulling on loose silk robes, Jed and Erik having stayed in the suite so often they both had changes of clothes there.

She had to roll up the sleeves on the one she was wearing, and it fell to her feel, but the silk was smooth, soft and surprisingly warm against her skin.

Connor called to order breakfast and the newspapers – local and financial - from the deli down the street as he usually did, his arm around Cherry's waist keeping her from going anywhere as the delivery boy arrived with the food, riding the private elevator up to the suite.

The silk robe slid off one thigh. When she tried to pull it back up, Connor snared her wrist.

Giving him a look, she said, "Connor."

He just grinned, unrepentant, shrugging.

The kid, a college student, couldn't take his eyes off her, off her full breasts beneath the silk robe ripe. Deliberately, Connor played with them, sliding his hands over the rich curves. He loved playing with them and got a kick out of the delivery boy's fascination.

Amused at both of them, Cherry rolled her eyes at him.

Her nipples hardened as Connor rubbed his palms over them and whispered in her ear. "Liked that, did you?"

She gave him a dry look and shook her head at him.

He just laughed.

Playing with her though and watching the hot look the delivery boy gave them, Connor was getting hard beneath the thin silk robe, his erection pressing against her firm bottom.

This was more fun than he'd had in years.

Deliberately, he pressed his mouth against her slender throat, sucking on it as he pinched her nipples lightly.

Seemingly oblivious to the kid staring, Jed paid him as Erik opened the Styrofoam packages.

The smell of food — bacon, eggs and toast filled the room.

Cherry's stomach growled.

The aromas were making them all hungry. She'd already had quite a workout and had probably worked up an appetite to match. She was probably starving. As they were.

Brushing her hair back from her throat, Connor brushed his thumb over the mark on her throat, admiring his handiwork and smiled. All three of them had left their brands on her. Love bites decorated her slender throat, marking her as theirs.

Cherry squirmed, looking at him, but he only tightened his arms around her a little.

"Connor," she said, "I'm hungry."

"First, we have a rule around here," he said, sliding her gently off his lap, pushing her lightly to her knees in front of him. "What one gets the others get. You'll have to sing for your breakfast first."

While she had eaten Erik, she hadn't actually swallowed with either Connor or Jed.

His cock was hard, rising at the thought of her going down on him, at the vision of Cherry on her knees in front of him, her drying hair haloing her face. With her curling blonde hair and blue eyes it was like fucking an angel. A naked angel but an angel all the same.

Looking down into those blue eyes and the speculative look that she gave him, he could also see that the idea excited her a little. He shifted forward, spreading his legs to give her access to his throbbing cock.

It had risen to the occasion.

Strangely, as Connor pulled his robe away from his throbbing and erect cock, the head already purple and engorged, the shaft rigid, Cherry's pussy tightened and flooded. The idea of servicing Connor this way was oddly stimulating. To her surprise her mouth watered at the idea, even as she looked at his long shaft and imagined it pumping his warm cum down her throat as Erik had.

Lifting an eyebrow, Cherry looked at Connor, considering it.

It wasn't as if they hadn't made her come multiple times.

His cock waited, twitching, so hard.

So did he, watching her with those brilliant blue eyes.

His cock was oddly beautiful, a primal thing.

Reaching out curiously, she ran her fingers down the length of it, the skin like the finest suede, soft and warm. A vein ran down it, pulsing.

Behind her, she could almost feel the weight of Jed and Erik's eyes on her, watching.

She opened her mouth and slowly took the head of Connor's cock between her lips, sucking on it obediently, curling her hand around the shaft. It swelled beneath her hand as she took him inside her mouth.

Carefully Cherry took the broad mushroom head deeper to get more used to him as he and Jed had done the night before, sliding her mouth up and down his shaft, tasting him, tasting Connor, sweeping her tongue around the glans, taking him a little deeper each time. He grew harder and harder in her mouth.

Looking up, she could see his eyes go unfocused, his gaze turn inward.

She would have smiled if she could but her mouth was too full.

His long fingers slid into her hair.

Cherry sighed.

Dropping his hands onto her head, Connor groaned as her hot mouth closed around him but didn't push, knowing her inexperience and letting her set her own pace at first, trying to guide her.

Watching her golden head bobbing over his cock, her long hair brushing against his thighs with each motion of her mouth on him, her full breasts swaying, was marvelously sensual.

He looked at Jed and Erik, their breakfasts forgotten as they watched Cherry deep throat him. They were riveted by the spectacle.

The sensation of her hot wet mouth on his cock was intense, brilliant.

His hands closed around her head, needing more, guiding her rhythm more firmly, trying to take her deeper carefully. Her throat tightened around him as he did and she struggled with it, something that was exciting in itself. He took her closer with the next thrust, deeper with the next.

Her throat working against the head of his cock shredded his control.

"Take a deep breath, Cherry," Connor said, hoarsely, pulling back long enough for her to do that.

She drew in a breath quickly, as his hands closed around her head.

Control shattered.

Connor thrust into her mouth hard, his hands clenched in her hair, going fast, deep and hard, using her mouth ruthlessly as she writhed and groaned.

He came, his hands clenched in her hair, pouring into her throat as she twisted, swallowing, each motion of her throat working him so that he gushed into her.

Frantically Cherry kept swallowing, taking him, taking everything he gave her as his cock went deep.

She sighed, sagging against him when he released her. Connor stroked her hair, her head against his thigh as she caught her breath. Her hair was soft and it rippled beneath his hand, he loved the feel of it, like silk. Idly, he fingered a strand.

That had been incredible. Brilliant.

She was definitely a quick learner.

"Are you all right?" he asked.

Taking a deep breath, she looked up at him and licked the last of his cum from her lips.

His body twitched in response.

She nodded, a small smile curving her mouth.

"Good," Jed said, "my turn, then, if you don't mind, Cherry."

Looking up at him, she said, shrugging a little, still smiling, "I don't mind."

Settling in before him where he sat in the chair, she took his offered cock into her mouth with a little more confidence. His hands closed around her head, already so hard that he needed her to take him and quick.

"It's going to go fast, Cherry," he warned.

She looked up at him and nodded.

With his hands in her hair guiding her rhythm he drove hard, fast and as deep as he dared. His cock was already so hard that she was afraid he'd explode into her mouth before she was ready.

Careless of her muffled cries he fucked her mouth hard and deep.

He was coming…his hands clenched in her hair.

Cherry sensed it and took a quick breath as he thrust deeply into her mouth, bursting down her throat, filling it with his salty thick cum. His hands locked in her hair, holding her in place as he gushed down her throat. Frantically, she swallowed him.

"Damn," Jed said, the tone of his voice a little sick and apologetic as he released her hair, his jaw going tight as he released her. "Cherry…"

He stroked her hair as she let her cheek rest against his thigh, a little stunned.

"I didn't mean it to go like that," he said.

She smiled up at him. "I guess I need more practice."

Looking down at her, he shook his head and grinned. "More practice?" He took a breath. "You can practice on me any time you like."

Cherry laughed as he helped her to her feet.

To her surprise, though, Connor reached out and tugged her back into his lap.

"Coffee or orange juice?"

Not surprisingly, after all she had eaten she wasn't quite as hungry as she had been.

"Both," she said. She might not be as hungry, but she was thirsty. "I'm dying of thirst, and I need my morning coffee."

Looking at the three of them, settled comfortably in Connor's lap as they shared out the newspapers between them, Cherry reflected that it was oddly exciting and freeing to relinquish control like this, letting them do with her as they pleased.

Even so, she refused to be bored.

"Mine," she declared, snagging the front page of the local paper.

It surprised all three of them.

Connor was pleased that Cherry wasn't overawed by him, unlike many of the women he'd dated. Nor did she just parrot his opinions, or Jed or Erik's, back at him. She had her own thoughts and wasn't afraid to express them.

Throughout the day Cherry found there was a rare few minutes when one or the other of them wasn't touching her or playing with her in some way, kissing her, playing with her hair, tweaking a nipple, stroking her thigh. Or sucking on her neck as Connor was doing while they talked, read the newspapers and watched TV, the boys flipping through the channels as men do. It was a little strange to talk about current events while one of them played with her breast or with the delicate folds and tissues between her thighs.

Cherry cuddled in Connor's lap with his arms loosely around her, her cheek against the firm muscles of his chest. He wasn't as massively muscled as Erik but he still had an impressive set of pecs. They were surprisingly comfortable.

Erik had pulled her legs across his lap, Jed, sitting on the floor, had threaded his arm around one of them.

She ached pleasantly, her body hot and in a nearly constant state of arousal, her pussy dampening the robe but she could hardly complain.

It was hard to ignore the fact, though, that Connor was growing increasingly distracted as he lifted his head from where he had been nuzzling and sucking at her throat, his fingers brushing lightly over it, his lips moving over her ear almost affectionately.

She tried not to think too much about that. This couldn't last forever and she knew it.

Just as she tried not to notice how her heart wrenched a little as he stroked her arm, her breasts, one arm curled around her waist, clasping it lightly.

Gathering up her hair, Connor drew her head back a little with it to admire his handiwork, his fingers sliding over her breast, plucking lightly at her nipple, rolling it as she shivered.

That was one of the things he found so fascinating about Cherry, that she was so completely responsive. Another livid mark now matched the others on her slender white throat. Her neck was encircled with them, each of them having left their brand on her more than once.

Her legs were across Erik's lap and Connor watched as Erik played lightly with the tender tissues between her thighs, finger-fucking her teasingly now and then.

Cherry's hips alternately bucked or she shivered, soft gasps and moans escaping her no matter how much she tried to bite them back. The muscles in her stomach and thighs tightened and flexed.

He was grateful to her for that.

Despite that very pleasant distraction though, he found his mind drifting to the situation at O'Donnell International and his problems with the Board.

It seemed intractable, with no solution. He worried at it as a dog would with a bone.

Connor sighed, tightening his arms around her.

Even as her scent soothed him a little the problems at O'Donnell floated at the back of his mind.

It was his company. His family's company. An O'Donnell had run it since its inception. He wouldn't be the one to lose it.

As much as he tried to fight the thin thread of pain, of panic, he couldn't.

There was no sense talking about it to Jed and Erik, they had heard it a thousand times before. Neither of them could do anything about it, either.

Sitting on the floor, his back to the couch, his arm curled comfortably around one of pretty Cherry's shapely legs, stroking it occasionally, Jed couldn't help being aware of her, nearly naked in Conn's lap. Her hair had dried into a riot of golden waves that tumbled over her pretty shoulders and her ripe round breasts.

His cock was a little hard just looking at her but he was also finding himself waiting for those little glints of humor as they talked, for the flash of intelligence in her blue eyes as they'd discussed what they read in the paper.

She wasn't just a bimbo. He had figured that out quickly, as had Connor and Erik.

At the moment she was having a spirited debate with Erik over the quarterback of his favorite football team to Jed and Connor's amusement.

"But he consistently overthrows his receivers," she said.

Jed was grateful for the distraction she provided Connor. It would have been a tough weekend otherwise with everything that was going on at the office.

"She's got you there, Erik," he said.

He glanced up at Conn, suddenly noticing that his comments about the game on TV had dropped off, to see the distracted look in his eyes, Connor's mouth brushing lightly against Cherry's hair, frowning slightly.

Mentally, Jed swore.

The situation should have been simple, there should have been no question about Conn becoming CEO in his father's place, in his family's company, but it hadn't, and it wasn't. The Board was making things increasingly difficult, grudgingly giving Conn the title but in many ways running OI was like having two captains steering the boat in different directions, like a push me-pull you, with everyone trying to figure out who was steering.

It wouldn't have been so bad if Conn hadn't been the kind of man he was. To him OI was more than a trust, it was more than an inheritance passed down from his Irish great-grandfather, the man that Connor had been named for, who had built the company from the ground up with nothing but determination and an idea. It wasn't just a company to him, it was a responsibility and the people in it weren't just employees, they depended on him to lead them in the right direction. Especially in the current economy.

That was why this had been so important. Why none of them had time to go looking to score, to date. And why the party, and Cherry, had been a godsend.

Jed eyes went to Erik, who looked back at him a little grimly. Giving Erik a look, Jed lifted his chin in question. They needed a distraction and he knew just the one that would do it.

He grinned.

Glancing at Cherry he saw she had noticed Connor's distraction, too, her eyes meeting his curiously.

Cherry saw where Jed's glance went, from a distracted Connor to Erik and back to her again.

"I'm hungry," Jed said, bluntly, his grin getting wider as he saw the mild alarm flare in her eyes at his words.

Those words got Connor's attention. He straightened behind her as Jed slid his hands up her legs.

Cherry's breath caught, seeing that look in Jed's eyes. She knew that look. Jed had something in mind. She had no doubt that she'd enjoy it but *damn*.

Wrapping his legs around hers, Connor opened her to Jed, Connor's hands moving to her breasts to caress and to toy with her nipples.

That had definitely gotten his attention.

Oh fine, she thought, vaguely amused, *throw me under the damn bus.*

"Jed," she protested, trying not to laugh even as her pussy tightened. "I thought you were my friend."

"Yeah," Connor said, nibbling at her ear, sending goose bumps racing over her skin. "But he's my friend first."

She swallowed hard, knowing what was coming.

Jed just grinned, his brown eyes glinting mischievously.

Spread for Jed as she was, she had no choice. She looked at him as he shifted forward, his hands sliding further up her legs, opening her even more.

He just smiled before his eyes dropped to her exposed pussy and he reached for her.

Knowing what he was about to do to her, what that talented mouth and tongue were capable of, her pussy clenched and heat poured through her once again.

"You're going to kill me, you know," she said, accusingly, fighting both a smile and anticipation, playing the game they needed her to play. "Death by sex."

And she'd bend over and let them do it. Again and again. She loved what they did to her.

Jed licked his lips to see her displayed in front of him, sliding his hands up her smooth white thighs, massaging them lightly as he admired her beautiful pussy. Carefully, he slid his hands beneath her butt, shifted her to the perfect position for viewing, for tasting, for eating.

"But what a way to go, Cherry," he said, appreciatively.

His cock had grown much harder.

Now he was the one anticipating.

"You have the prettiest pussy, Cherry," he said, sliding a finger down between her blushing labia, her anticipation dampening her.

She wanted it, wanted what they would do to her, as much as she might pretend otherwise.

Deliberately, he parted those tender folds, held them and her clit open and exposed, blowing air lightly across them so that she would feel how exposed she was to him. So she would know it.

Cherry quivered.

Behind her Connor's attention was once more focused on the hot and sexy woman in his lap, looking down at Jed and grinning as Jed tormented her.

That was better.

Deliberately, Jed lowered his mouth to those plush lower lips, to Cherry's moist core and took a long deep taste of her, stroking his tongue into her pussy as he gently pushed her legs farther apart. His tongue slid up and across her clit as he teased her.

She moaned, her head falling back against Connor's shoulder. Perfect.

Connor took her soft mouth with his as Jed took her pussy the same way, Connor swallowing her moans and cries as she quivered.

Jed loved the sound of her pleasure, loved to watch her eyelids flutter as she surrendered to it, to him, her body theirs to command. Both Conn and Erik were apparently enjoying it as well, watching as she shook and trembled, Conn's mouth once more on her throat, Erik sucking on her tit, squeezing it while Conn toyed with the other.

As a distraction for Connor, for all of them, Cherry was just what the doctor had ordered. Jed could only be grateful for that.

He also loved watching her come, loved watching her muscles tremble, her body arch…

Cherry tightened, heat pooling in her belly as Jed ate her slowly, steadily and with evident and very real relish, his long, gifted tongue spearing into her again and again, sliding up to lap at and circle her clit. Electric sparks raced through her, heat following in their wake. Her body was no longer hers to command but Jed's, his darting, dancing tongue making her delirious, driving her insane as Connor and then Erik played with her breasts idly, pinching and tugging on her nipples. The muscles in her thighs and belly jumped with each flick of Jed's tongue along her clit.

Warmth filled her, a current of electric excitement spearing through her, knowing that they were probably going to fuck her again and wondering how.

One long finger slid up inside her, then another, scissoring. Three, stretching her so wide, wider, stroking as Jed sipped and licked at her clit, the small light motions of his mouth on her sending sharp bursts of intense pleasure soaring through her body.

A cry built in her throat as it took her over, as all thought vanished except for the touch of Jed's mouth on her, his soft wet tongue driving her up. His mouth closed over her clit, sucking hard, drawing it out to where his tongue could slide against it.

Heat exploded through her.

She erupted, her pussy gushing, Jed lapping and sucking at her as she wailed, arching, every muscle going rigid.

Connor thought he'd never felt anything quite so intoxicating as Cherry's fingers twitching around his cock as her body shuddered, quaking in his lap as she came, hard and fast.

"Cherry's a little wet," Erik commented, apparently idly, dipping a finger into Cherry's exposed cleft as Jed sat back and he glanced at the football game as the winning run was made. "I think someone needs fucked."

Sliding his fingers between her thighs to play, pinching her sensitized clit, sliding a finger inside her in his turn as she gasped and moaned softly, Connor could only nod. She was definitely hot and wet.

If she thought it had been good until now, he thought, *they had only just started.*

She was just what he needed to keep his mind off things.

A distraction.

"It's time to play," he said, watching Jed's eyes go hot and Erik grin.

Connor stood, yanked on Cherry's arm to toss her over his shoulder, giving her bottom a sharp smack as he settled her there.

"Don't wiggle too much, I don't want to drop you," he said.

She yelped a little in surprise but more so when he dumped her on the bed and Erik flipped her over on her belly, swiftly securing her hands once more behind her before turning her over once again. Then he and Jed each tied one of Connor's silk ties around her ankles, spreading her legs wide, her hips at the edge of the bed as they secured her to the legs.

Another tie was secured around her pretty blue eyes as a blindfold.

With her hands bound behind her back, it forced her to arch, presenting her full breasts to them. She couldn't escape, couldn't wriggle away, not with her ankles tied to the bed frame, and she couldn't see, so everything she experienced, every sensation, everything they did to her would be heightened, intensified.

This was another fantasy of theirs, to drive a woman completely insane with pleasure, until she was wet, dripping, begging to come, to be taken, to be used. To torment her until she was delirious, half out of her mind.

He nodded to Jed and Erik.

It would be wonderful to watch her twitch, tremble and shudder as they played with her.

Cherry was a toy. Their toy now to use as they pleased, listening to her sob, moan and wail as they teased her, watching her breasts swell, her juices pour out of her pussy, her body tremble and quiver.

And what a toy. She enjoyed it so much. Her voice rose and fell as they played, shifting from moan to groan, to soft cries that rose in pitch as she came close to a release they would not give her. Her body twisted and writhed, her breath caught and released, her muscles worked as need and desire drove her mindless, her hips pumping, quivering, begging for more. She trembled and twitched wildly. Helplessly.

All three of them were as hard as rocks but pleasuring her like this was intoxicating.

Her pretty lips parted in anticipation.

Fear was no longer an issue for Cherry, just curiosity. Blindfolded, she could only wonder what they would do to her next?

And then she found out.

Her belly tightened and her pussy flooded as she heard the sound of a nightstand drawer rattling, being opened, a shuffling inside it and then the soft buzz of vibrators.

One of them touched her intimately. Then another. The blindfold seemed to intensify each touch, each sensation.

A vibrator caressed Cherry's tender clit, teased and tormented it while another played around her pussy lips. Someone sucked and suckled on her nipples until they were taut, aching, before something hard closed on them, first one, then the other, locked on them, pinching them with a mix of pain and delicious pleasure. A quick tug pulled on both at once and she moaned. Something touched her clit and buzzed tantalizingly. Vibrators teased at her pussy until she was dripping, moaning.

In what seemed like moments Cherry was long past thought. She was on fire, her skin was hot, the little vibrator teasing her clit hummed, driving her mad as pleasure coursed from it to her pussy.

Close, hovering on the edge, but not over it.

Against her will she whimpered.

"Tell us…Beg for it," a deep voice whispered in her ear, his lips sending shivers over her.

She knew that voice.

"Please, oh God, please, Connor…"

The vibrators danced on her clit, slipped and slid just inside her pussy, teasing in and out. maddeningly.

"Not yet…," that soft voice said.

She wailed in frustration, wanting, needing to come.

A huge hard dildo slid up inside her cunt, someone stroking it deep into her.

"Are you hot?" Connor said, in her ear, as the buzzing on her clit intensified, then eased.

Her pussy clenched around the dildo, around the hard unyielding plastic within her.

"Connor, please," she gasped. "Yes…"

Someone worked the dildo inside her, fucking her with it. She went blind with need, a haze washing over her darkened vision as the pleasure from her clit and the dildo inside her drowned her.

"Do you want to come?"

"Yes, Connor. Please."

"Not yet."

Cherry nearly wept with need.

Something probed at her ass, the vibration telling, before it slid inside her. Her whole body quivered once it was seated deep within.

The speed on the slender vibrator went up and she moaned. Pleasure and heat swept through her in wave after wave, the muscles of her belly tightened, her thighs twitched. It was sweet delicious torture.

"Please, dear God, Connor," she whimpered, "please."

"No, only when I tell you."

All thought vanished.

For a moment Connor stood back to watch, all three of them pausing to look at Cherry's lovely body quivering helplessly, her thighs wet, both nipples tight and distended as Erik reattached the nipple clamps to them and tugged on them lightly to hear her moan. She was beautiful, color washing beneath her skin. A dildo was inside her pussy as Connor played the clit vibrator across her, her body twitching wildly with each touch of it.

Her every breath sobbed.

His cock was hard and tight, so much so that he was ready to cream all over those gorgeous breasts. He was tempted but he wanted her tight heat around him. He really wanted to fuck her.

Gently, Connor stroked a hand over her satiny skin, the muscles beneath it jumping.

"Beg," he said.

"Please," Cherry whimpered.

"Not yet. When I tell you..."

"Cherry," Jed said and rubbed his cock against her parted lips.

Like a baby bird, her mouth opened to take him.

Connor went rock hard.

Watching Cherry as her body trembled and shook, her mouth locked hungrily around Jed's cock while Erik sucked hard at one of her ripe breasts, was like watching their favorite fantasy come to life. She was beautiful, her body a wonderland, a marvelous toy for them to play with. It was amazing that she was willing to let them do as they would with her.

Working the vibrator lightly over her clit, Connor reached for the dildo, fucking her with it again. She groaned with need, her hips pumping, lifting and falling.

Connor watched Jed's face, his body going rigid with pleasure as his cock plunged in and out of Cherry's sweet mouth. It was something to watch one of his best friends getting off.

He'd give Jed a little help.

Looking at the expression on Jed's face, Connor grinned, rock hard and ready to come himself.

"Now," he said.

He danced the vibrator on her clit, thrusting the dildo inside her.

Cherry quivered, twisted, trying to escape, trying to find release, her hips pumping as he teased her. She was a pool of need, moaning, pleading.

He settled the vibrator on her clit and Cherry moaned, the sound rising until she cried out around Jed's swollen cock in her mouth, her body shivering, shuddering, clenching, her orgasm seemingly endless as she quivered.

The vibration of her moan and then her shriek around his cock, hearing the sound of it, watching her body quiver and shake, was more than Jed could stand, it seemed. His hands locked in her hair as he came with a ragged shout.

The sound of it, watching Jed empty into her mouth, was more than Connor could stand, too, it seemed.

He drove his throbbing cock deep inside her, inside Cherry's hot and drenched pussy, her body clenching around him, the vibrator in her ass adding another layer to his ecstasy. He pounded into her, lost in the glorious tight heat of her, battering at her. She was so very tight, so hot, her internal muscles closing around him gloriously.

This was what he had needed, to stop thinking for a little while, to just feel. He was astonishingly grateful for it as he pounded into her, into sweet Cherry.

A cock slammed up inside her and Cherry cried out in surprise and pleasure around the one in her mouth as one of them fucked her hard and fast, pounding into her. She came, intensely, after all the torment. Her orgasm was a hot fist slamming through her as thick cum filled her mouth and then her pussy. Frantically she swallowed.

They gave her no respite.

Every part of her body still quivering, the sweet torture began again, Cherry's head tossing as they suckled and fondled her, teased and tormented, another thick cock in her mouth. Every part of her body was used and invaded until her muscles were jumping and her pussy was dripping again. Then the next took her, her body bucking with the force of it as he pounded into her, groaning.

"Beg."

"Please…"

Erik, his thick member unmistakable inside her as he took her hard and deep, each thrust pulling against her bound legs.

He didn't come, although he groaned and swelled inside her with pleasure.

Coming he saved for her mouth. His thick cock invaded that as Connor's slid into her ass and filled her.

By the time they were done with her, she was limp, trembling and utterly exhausted.

Tenderly and gently, they removed the blindfold and untied her.

Finally. It was a huge relief to her shoulders.

"Are you all right?" Connor asked, a little worriedly, pulling her up into his arms.

She smiled weakly but reassuringly and nodded, touched by his concern, brushing a hand over his strong chest, relieved to finally be able to do it, finding comfort as his arms closed around her, blowing out a shaky breath as the three of them curled up around her.

For the first time in her life she could safely say that she was completely and utterly sated.

And exhausted for the second straight night in a row. For the first time in a long time she was finally getting enough sleep.

With Connor, Jed and Erik curling up around her, she closed her eyes.

Chapter Six

Hard male bodies surrounded her. That wasn't bad. A mouth was wrapped around each nipple, another was buried between her thighs. Lifting her a little, a pillow was pushed underneath her hips. The mouth settled in to savor her. Given the talent, it had to be Jed. Juices flooded her pussy. That gifted tongue was deliciously deep inside her, licking her pussy, sucking on it, sucking her juices from within her until she moaned, her eyes still closed.

That warm mouth moved up, found her clit, savored, sucked, as fingers slid where the tongue had been, both stroking steadily, the mouths on her nipples suckling with increasing pressure, all three of them easing her up and up. When she came it was in a long slow roll of pleasure, of ecstasy, a soft cry escaping her as her body shuddered, glory moving through it.

When she dared to open her eyes, she found Jed with his head pillowed on her thigh, licking his lips with satisfaction, Connor and Erik to each side, Connor's hand curled around a breast, Erik running a finger lightly around inside her navel.

Rolling her shoulders to ease the stiffness, she smiled, running the backs of her hands over the firm muscles of their chests, Connor's firm and hard, Erik's unbelievably broad, before reaching down to brush back Jed's hair with a contented sigh.

She murmured, "You feel wonderful. I love touching you, all of you."

A shiver of pleasure shot through Connor as her warm hand brushed across his chest, her hand curling over the muscle, stroking. She smiled as she touched him and something in that look, in the pure pleasure she took in touching him, stirred something inside him as no one and nothing else ever had.

"We'll have to do something about getting you some clothes," Connor said.

Cherry smiled wryly. "There should be a package on your desk in your office. Patrick would have sent something for afterward, in case something happened."

With the lift of an eyebrow, Connor gave her a questioning look.

She sighed and gave him a look right back. Her tone was kind, a little apologetic, and that twisted something inside him.

"Don't take this badly, Connor, but your reputation preceded you. All of you. I didn't go into this completely blindly. Patrick and I both knew that something might happen."

"You wanted it?"

Clearly his reputation didn't bother her but surprisingly with her it did bother him. He didn't want her to think that any of this had been casual or meaningless. She had fulfilled a long-time fantasy of theirs.

Those beautiful blue eyes looked at him, a little uncomfortably.

Cherry shrugged, a little uncomfortable. "I only thought it would be fun, a lark, to help Patrick… I wasn't expecting…all this…"

With a wave, she looked from one to the other of them.

"I wondered, maybe… it was a fantasy… but this?"

So, it had been her fantasy, too, and not just theirs. There was something to that.

Connor went down to his silent, empty office and out to his secretary's desk.

He found a package waiting there.

A long moment went by as he looked at it, turning the implications of it over in his mind.

He returned shortly after with the soft, twine wrapped package.

When she made no move to open it, setting it aside instead, Jed said, "Don't you want to get dressed?"

Both Connor and Erik waited for her answer, knowing that dressing probably meant that she was leaving and they were loath for her to leave. Not to mention covering up that lovely lush body.

But Connor even more so.

She looked at Jed, at Erik. It was Sunday, and early.

"Not yet, particularly. Do you want me to?"

A slow smile spread across Jed's face as he shook his head. "I'm in no hurry."

Something loosened in Connor, too, knowing she was as reluctant to leave as he was for her to go. He was aware she wasn't looking at him and also aware that she was making the effort not to. He knew that look, he'd seen it before. She wanted to stay, but was giving him space in case it wasn't what he wanted.

It wasn't.

Tossing the package out of his way, he dove across the bed, to ravage her breasts while she laughed, kissed her senseless and then rolled off the bed toward the bathroom.

Relaxing a little, he called to order breakfast and went to shave, already feeling lighter.

As the delivery boy arrived with breakfast, Jed pulled Cherry into his lap. She went into it willingly while Connor shaved and Erik showered.

She stroked his chest with obvious fascination and evident enjoyment, her hands molding against the muscles of his chest. The pleasure of her hands on him was incredibly gratifying. Jed enjoyed the attention thoroughly, soaking up the sweet sensation of her touch, relishing her obvious delight as her fingers skimmed over him. No other woman had ever done anything like it or even come close.

The delivery boy's eyes popped even further as Jed wrapped an arm around her to keep her in his lap as he paid the kid, the boy watching with fascination even as he returned to the elevator.

"Exhibitionist," Jed said, gently, smiling.

Equably, she answered, her hands running over him again, frowning a little in concentration but clearly amused. "Did you miss how we met?"

Remembering her stretched out naked and covered in chocolate he had to grin.

"True," he said, chuckling, shifting her a little, his parted robe allowing his hardening cock to brush across her damp pussy.

Standing, smiling, Cherry straddled him, his hard erection pressing at her slit as she slowly lowered herself onto him, looking him steadily in the eyes as she did. Her hot, tight wetness closed around the head of his rigid cock.

Meeting her beautiful blue eyes, Jed brushed the hair back from her face with both hands. Cupping her face between his hands he kissed her gently, thrusting up inside her to fill her.

She smiled as he entered her, as he slid inside her and at that smile something around his heart shifted and moved.

They rocked together, he and Cherry, pleasure building slowly. When she came, she buried her face against his shoulder, muffling her cry of satisfaction against his skin, her juices flooding over cock.

Jed held her as he went tight, groaning as he came, too, and erupted into her moist delicious heat.

He held her that way, her head on his shoulder, until they heard Connor and Erik coming and then he released her.

They each gave Cherry a kiss before they found their own seats, Connor pulling her into his lap as they shared out breakfast and the newspaper.

Erik caught up with her when Cherry went to take her turn in the shower, lifting her into his powerful arms without comment or warning, his hands cupped around the globes of her ass, pressing her against the wall as his thick cock slid up inside her. She took his strong square face in her hands and kissed him lightly, moaning as his broad shaft filled her. He cocked her gently but deeply as she wrapped her legs around his waist, his hands curled beneath her butt, spreading her so that he could thrust into her more deeply.

He watched her pleasure take her, color washing through her fair skin, filling her with his hot cum as she cried out, quivering in his arms, his face against her throat as he groaned with his own release.

For a moment, he leaned against her weakly, his legs trembling from his orgasm, pressing her against the cool tiles. She stroked his hair.

Erik sighed, looking into her eyes as he let her down. "I love fucking you, Cherry, I can't seem to get enough of you. None of us can."

"I love it, too," she said.

She did, even though she was a little sore from all the attention.

He left her to take her shower.

The shower was state of the art, with those multiple spray heads and jets triggered by remote and a rainwater simulator above. The warm water felt wonderful as it sluiced over her, the jets pulsing against Cherry's abused muscles. It should have felt better but her heart was oddly heavy. It was beginning to seem a lot like it was time to say goodbye.

She would have to leave soon one way or the other anyway, she knew. Real life waited outside and she would have to go back to it. She had a job and a job to do. Her little sexual mini-vacation had to come to an end sooner or later, as much as she suddenly found herself wishing otherwise.

It was ridiculous to think they might want her to stay with them, to keep all three of them. Ridiculous maybe, but she did.

As she'd said, though, she knew their reputations. They were playboys, a different set of women every night. By all accounts when they partied they partied hard.

And none of them had asked.

But damn, to her shock she found she would miss them, sweet Jed with his soulful eyes and talented mouth, quiet reserved Erik and his powerful arms.

And Connor, with his inventive mind, his comfortable lap and his incredibly blue eyes.

To her astonishment and dismay her eyes were burning.

She took a long slow breath, then let it out just as slowly, stepping out of the shower and tossing her hair over her head to patiently comb out the myriad tangles they had put in it when they made her toss and turn so much.

The soothing motion, the familiar habit, helped ground her again, helped keep her in the here and now.

She didn't hear Connor walk quietly into the bathroom behind her.

That was the view of Cherry Connor saw when he walked in, bent over naked, the water from her shower still beading her soft skin, her lovely body bent nearly in half, her long hair almost touching the floor as she combed it out with her fingers, her full breasts swaying, her pretty bottom turned his way.

She had an amazing ass, rounded but firm.

He went hard and hot in an instant, frozen briefly at the sight of her standing there like that.

She looked like some kind of water nymph from a fairy story, beautiful, innocently erotic despite all they had done with and to her. What he wanted to do to her again.

All he wanted was her, lust and something else slamming through him.

He said nothing, the only warning she had was when he rammed his cock deeply into her tight pussy, his hands locked on her hips to hold her in place. She gasped with surprise before she arched her back in pleasure.

She was delicious, wonderful, so tight, so wet and he just wanted more of her.

Connor pounded into her, hammered into that sweet pussy as it closed tightly around him.

He ran a hand up her lovely back, the muscles flexing as she took his battering thrusts.

Tossing her hair back over her shoulder, startled at first by the sudden invasion Cherry braced herself against the counter to take Connor's erotic assault, looking at him in the mirror as he pounded into her, his expression unreadable, his square jaw tight, his blue eyes blazing as he took her. He looked incredible, intense, every muscle taut.

His cock throbbed, swelling inside her as he battered into her, the sound of flesh striking flesh rhythmic.

Turning her head, she looked back over her shoulder at him as he thrust and hammered into her, pleasure slamming through her with each hard punch of his cock into her.

Grabbing a handful of her hair, Connor dragged her head back and up and buried his mouth at the curve of her jaw. Even as her heart wrenched at that intimate touch, he plunged into her. His other hand he filled with her breast, squeezing hard, almost painfully, his fingers tight on her nipple. In response to his torment Cherry arched into his touch, her arms braced, her pussy clutched around his raging cock, her body begging for more as he slammed into it, into her, with more and more force. His free hand slid down to torment her clit.

"Come for me, Cherry," he whispered in her ear, his voice low and hoarse.

As if at his command, she did, crying out, her body reacting as he fucked her so hard and deeply she grunted with the impact of each punishing slam of his hips against hers, quivering as she closed around him, pulsing, shuddering. Heat raced under her skin.

The slick internal muscles of her pussy gloved Connor tightly and stroked him, milking him deliciously. He came with a long low moan, pumping into her, ecstasy rushing through him seemingly endlessly, filling her as he drew her against his chest and held her there tightly, his arms banded around her chest and stomach, his face against her hair.

Cherry turned her face into his chest to press her cheek against it as Connor wrapped his arms around her.

They didn't move apart until his cock slid out of her.

Connor turned her, looking down into her lovely face, into her brilliant blue eyes.

Very, very softly, he kissed her, taking her mouth deeply, sweetly, his tongue and hers twining. Something he didn't recognize moved through him as her hands swept over his chest, up over his shoulders, caressing him, curling around his head as her mouth moved beneath his. The kiss deepened, intensified.

A different kind of warmth moved through him.

He couldn't say the words he needed to say.

Then Erik called him from the other room.

Connor stroked her cheek, briefly, kissed her lightly.

"I'll let you finish drying your hair," he said with a satisfied grin.

The sound of the elevator descending a few moments later was unmistakable. They found the paper her clothes had been wrapped in, empty, in Connor's bedroom.

Cherry was gone.

It suddenly occurred to him that he didn't know her full name. There were things he had wanted to say to her, but hadn't. It was probably for the best, though. This way there would be no awkward goodbyes, no promises made that couldn't be kept.

Or so Connor tried to tell himself.

He looked at Jed and Erik. They were both quiet, still. He took a breath, regret washing through him. Their idyll was done.

Now he wished, suddenly and intensely, that it wasn't.

Chapter Seven

Each rise and fall of the elevator had been sheer torture, but finally Patrick heard Cherry coming home as the elevator rose and the doors opened onto their floor. He popped out of his apartment as soon as he heard her key rattling in the lock of her door across the hall. He'd been waiting for her. That was how they had first met and become friends in the first place, she lived in the apartment across the hall from him. Their occasional conversations and meetings in the hall and elevators had turned into a real friendship.

When he had returned to the dining room at O'Donnell International the next morning with his staff to clean up, knowing he hadn't heard her come home, he had wondered with one of them had taken him up on his suggestion. Or what had might have happened. But he didn't *know*. (Part of him was also a little worried, although he didn't want to admit that) And he didn't know who, how much, how many. He had left the bag with her clothes and wallet in it on Connor O'Donnell's secretary's desk.

She had been gone the whole weekend, though, and curiosity was killing him.

"Well," he said, archly, pleased at least that she'd gotten some part of her fantasy, knowing she had daydreamed about Connor O'Donnell or his friends Jed and Erik, for a while — well, so had he now and then, as much as he loved Alan — "look what the cat *finally* dragged in. Did you have good time?"

His eyebrows lifted as she turned at the sound of his door opening and he caught sight of her neck.

To his amusement, she blushed as she saw where his eyes went.

He snickered. "Either you did or you were attacked by a swarm of very hungry vampires."

"That'll be hard to hide," Alan commented, chuckling as he came to the door, too, leaning a shoulder against the jamb. "So, I guess you had a good time?"

Cherry turned to look at him and grinned a little wryly, having caught more than a few looks on the street as she summoned a taxi. Not to mention she ached all over, inside and out, not entirely unpleasantly, although it did hurt a little to walk too hard or too fast. The brush of her bra over her abused nipples made them ache.

Shrugging, a little abashed, Cherry said with a grin. "That's what they invented scarves for."

"C'mon in and dish, girlfriend," Patrick said. "I want to hear all about it. So, who was it?"

She looked at him over her shoulder as he held the door for her to pass and dropped her bomb, knowing it was safe with him and Alan.

"Well, you know how I told you that people at the company say Connor shares everything with Jed and Erik?" she said, "He does and they do share *everything*."

"Everything," Patrick stammered and then said, his voice stunned but almost admiring, as he followed her, "All three of them? Holy shit, girlfriend, how are you even walking?"

Not easily or well and sitting was even worse, although she really couldn't complain, except for the way it had ended.

Taking a deep breath, Cherry remembered watching Connor walk out of the bathroom, tall, handsome, lean. Her heart twisted. She'd had her fantasy and she had the aches to prove it. But that was what it was, a fantasy and she had known that.

It had had to end.

Whether they had known it or not, they had all been saying goodbye. She knew she had to go before it became impossible for her to leave without acting stupid, without tears.

Her heart wrenched but she pushed it aside. She'd known exactly what she was getting into, had walked into it with eyes wide open. It was ridiculous to complain about it now.

"Tell me everything," Patrick said, gleefully.

Alan looked into her eyes and touched her hand.

She gave him a reassuring smile.

It was hours before she finally managed to walk into her empty apartment, after having told them as much as she dared.

There were some details that you just didn't share, like being tied up, although now she could say that she could understand the pleasure Patrick and Alan took in each other. As close as they were, though, she, Patrick and Alan, there some things that she just couldn't say to even them. Like that she had started becoming attached to them, to Connor's assertiveness and flashes of kindness, to Jed's intense desire to please, Erik's strength both internally and externally. To all three of them with their desire not only to share her but to share with her…

For the first time since she'd moved there, her apartment seemed strange and empty.

She sighed. It would pass in time, she knew.

The scent of Connor was still on her skin, she could smell the scent of his cum on her. She changed into other clothes, clothes that didn't have his scent on them — nothing that would remind her of the weekend.

She missed them. That was something that she would never admit to Patrick, either, although she sensed that both he and Alan guessed.

Out of habit and old routine she checked her voice and e-mail.

Then she settled down to answer the more urgent e-mails, pulling out her attaché to review the briefs in it, multi-tasking, burying herself in work, using it to distract her as she always did.

If her heart ached as much as her tired, well-used body did, she put it aside. She hadn't asked for forever but a part of her wished…

It had been an incredible experience, though.

She just wished that she could repeat it.

Opening another e-mail, she went still, frowning and sighed.

It seemed that even if she wanted to, she not only couldn't but shouldn't and wouldn't even if she could.

Chapter Eight

It was no way to end a week. Almost three weeks had passed since the party Connor had thrown when he'd been formally acknowledged as C.E.O. and he was already ready to throw something. The first thing he would throw being the papers in his hand, his hand tightening around them, crumpling them in his fist. Both Jed and Erik braced themselves for the explosion. It was the coffee cup, though, that died a noble death, sailing across the room to shatter against the windows.

Not that either Jed or Erik, both watching, blamed him.

"The Board is calling for a vote of no-confidence," Connor said, tightly. "The meeting is this afternoon."

It was a complete surprise, not even a rumor of it had reached him. Nor had they given him any time to prepare. It wasn't even the first time a CEO had been booted from his own company there was certainly precedent for it.

Word hadn't reached Jed, either. He'd been too busy putting his own people in place as well as putting out other corporate fires, so he didn't had time to take the pulse of the corporation yet. It was clear by the tightening of his jaw that he was furious with himself. Not that that was any excuse as far as he was concerned, Connor knew.

"It's not your fault, Jed," Connor said. "Stop kicking yourself for not seeing it coming. I didn't see it coming either. We all knew that they wanted my father, or someone more like him, not me."

"There were rumors, but I hadn't nailed it down yet."

Connor certainly didn't blame Jed, most of those in the company knew that Jed was his friend, so they would have taken pains to make sure he didn't find out or risk letting Connor get his wind up.

They would offered him a buyout, he noted bitterly, to give up his family's company, a quite generous sum no doubt but on his twenty-first birthday Connor had inherited an even bigger one from the trust his great-grandfather had set up. The one who had built the company. The one he had been named after. Who had left his legacy in Connor's trust.

"It hasn't even been a month," Connor said, his jaw tight, "How much did they expect me to accomplish in so little time?"

Especially with the Chairman of the Board, a job that should also have been his when he was named CEO, getting in his way, making decisions without consulting him and giving contradictory orders.

Connor had wanted the transition from his father to himself to go easily, to move carefully, to make it easy on everyone, not charge in like a bull or the heir apparent arrogantly taking the throne. They had carefully planned it out but if this succeeded he wouldn't have the chance to put the rest of those plans into action.

And he'd be booted out of the company his great-grandfather started.

His family's company.

It was everything to him, virtually a part of him, something he had grown up with, his legacy, entrusted to him. As a boy he'd worked in the mail room, working his way up through the company so he would know it, every inch of it, intimately.

He stalked to the windows, frustration and fury evident in every line of his body.

Outside of cleaning out some deadwood and hiring Patrick Monaghan as their corporate chef, he hadn't had much time to do more than that. The memory of how Monaghan had gotten his position washed through him and with it the memory of Cherry. His body tightened. Even at a time like this he found he couldn't get her out of his mind.

Neither, he knew, could Jed or Erik.

Their nights out consisted of trying to find someone like her, someone they could share and play with as they had her. So far, with no luck.

Oddly enough, they all missed her, even after only knowing her for that brief time.

It had been enough to know that she shared their sense of adventure, that she was warm and affectionate, that she was willing and curious—intelligent, too, remembering their conversations—as well as eager and as highly sexed as they were, capable of keeping up with all three of them and more than willing to indulge them. At one and the same time.

There were times when he thought they had lost their only chance.

He couldn't help but wonder, too, why she had left when it had seemed that she had been enjoying herself as much as they were.

Watching his eyes, Jed could tell where Connor's thoughts had gone as his friend looked out the window. Even in the midst of all this, or maybe because of it.

Missing Cherry, too, Jed had finally gone to Patrick Monaghan for answers.

His eyes clearly pained, Patrick had shaken his head when Jed had brought it up.

"I'll tell her that you were asking," he'd said, "but it's up to Cherry to answer. There are reasons, very good reasons why she can't talk to any of you right now."

That was all that he would say on it, but he was clearly conflicted.

If Connor lost his position at OI, both Jed and Erik knew that it was likely that they would, too, not that either of them cared about that so much. They wouldn't have stayed if he went anyway.

But they wouldn't be losing their legacy.

Jed said, "You've got a whole stable of attorneys here. Maybe you should talk to them, Conn."

With a sigh Connor said, "I already called them. After the two of you, they were my next call. They'll be here any minute."

His secretary knocked at the door.

Fiftyish, matronly, Beth looked after him much like his own mother had before she had died. Connor had still been in high school. Beth's round face was pale, her lips tight with unhappiness and disapproval. Her warm brown eyes were glinting with righteous indignation and anger.

"They're here, sir."

"Send them in," he said.

With a nod, she stood aside.

Looking at the bunch of them file in wearing their dull gray, black or dark blue suits, their faces mostly grim, those in the lead mostly over fifty, white, heavy and primarily male, Connor thought that they were the prime example of everything that was wrong with corporations. A whole bunch of people whose main purpose was to say, No, you can't. A phalanx of assistants, aides, toadies and sycophants followed them, sitting in chairs and lining the windows behind those at the conference table.

Each of them had a copy of everything he had.

Taking his seat at the head of the conference room table, gesturing Jed and Erik to seats on either side of him, Connor leaned back in his chair.

"All right, what are my options?"

The senior attorney, Marcus Warren leaned forward, clasped his hands and looked at him steadily. "It depends on what is most important to you. Right now the last thing the company needs in the wake of your father's death is a proxy fight."

It wouldn't exactly be a proxy fight, which Connor well knew. The company was still privately owned. It would be a battle between Connor, those he thought he could influence on the Board and the remaining members. Should word get out about it, though, confidence in the company would be shaken. OI's competition would move in on their clients, and with reason if the management was at war with each other.

Something they both knew.

Taking a breath, Marcus Warren said, settling into his chair, his hands folded on his expansive belly. "I'd advise you to take the offer."

Connor sat back, looking at the man. "That's not the recommendation that I'm looking for."

"Mr. O'Donnell," Warren said, with small almost apologetic shrug, "You're relatively wealthy. It's unlikely that you'll survive the no-confidence vote. Taking the offer will save you embarrassment. No one would blame you if you accepted the offer as stated here. It's quite handsome."

"The offer you helped to craft," a voice said evenly but sharply from among those seated along the window.

Warren shot a look over his shoulder.

"Miss Stratford," he said, repressively.

She stood, a cool distant blonde, briefcase in hand, the epitome of everything Connor hated about corporate women.

Her hair was drawn back smoothly and tightly into a neat French twist, not a hair of it out of place, her eyes hidden behind serious horn-rimmed glasses, her boxy suit designed to conceal her body. Her makeup was a powdered and perfect mask, turning her skin to porcelain, a dusting of blusher across her cheekbones, her mouth coated with raisin colored lipstick. Only the shoes on her feet, the heels at least three inches high, belied the strict and conforming dress code. Her back was very straight, her chin lifted just so.

He did notice she had great legs for a lawyer.

"Mr. O'Donnell," she said, ignoring her superior and looking at Connor. "The gentlemen here represent the company, not you. Many of those here were asked by the Board to craft that very opinion you have in your hands. They hardly have your best interests at heart."

"Sit down, Miss Stratford," Warren said sharply, visibly alarmed.

Ignoring him she turned to Connor.

"If you want to keep your company, Mr. O'Donnell," she said, "take me with you to the meeting of the Board."

"And you are?"

She looked at him. "C.J. Stratford."

Disdainfully, Warren said, "Miss Stratford, what is it you think you know?"

Her smile turned sweetly cold, a mere curve of lips. "More than you do. You missed something. I tried to tell you that you couldn't do it. You didn't listen."

There was a certainty to her, a calm confidence. Connor gambled.

"Miss Stratford, please stay," Connor said, "the rest of you can leave."

When the room was empty of all but himself, Jed, Erik and the lawyer, he said, "What do you advise?"

Those eyes behind the glasses looked at him squarely. She smiled, albeit a little grimly.

"First," she said, "you'll have to trust me. With all due respect to your late father, he allowed the Board too much power. They've grown accustomed to it."

That had been his own opinion.

Connor eyed her. He looked at Jed and Erik. Both shrugged.

In the end what choice did he have?

Chapter Nine

The company boardroom was of a piece with the rest of the corporate floors, lavish and expensively furnished, the inner walls paneled here in oak, a plush carpet, the outer walls a broad expanse of windows that looked out over the city. Along one wall Patrick Monaghan's people had laid out a buffet. The air of the room was full of the scent of garlic and other spices.

Connor hadn't been able to eat.

Having finished their luncheon courtesy of the company, the Board had gathered and taken their seats at the conference room table in the company boardroom, a group of about a dozen men and one token woman, not including Connor, Jed and Erik, when C.J. Stratford walked into the room.

It seemed she had taken the time after their meeting in the morning to change clothes. Into another suit, yes, but it was a still a marked change, the color a light buttery yellow, so that she was like a beam of sunlight among all the dark suits, drawing eyes to her.

She walked confidently into the room as if she were six inches taller, her stride even as she entered and seemingly unaware of the unfriendly eyes on her as she walked to join Connor at the head of the table. As aware as she must be that she gambled with not just his position at the company but her career if she lost, she gave no sign of it.

Connor hadn't missed that fact, either. She was taking as big a gamble as he was. Another reason why he had taken the chance with her.

As she went around the conference table she handed each person sitting there an envelope.

Taking the chair behind him in her position as his advisor and attorney, she leaned forward to whisper in his ear.

"Trust me," she said again, reassuringly.

It was a hell of a risk he was taking but he had no real choice, not if the company his grandfather had founded was to survive.

Few companies did well after those who were invested in them were gone — for whatever reason.

The Board meeting started with its usual opening, a reading of the minutes and such, a secretary recording the meeting as well by hand into a computer. Everyone looked at Connor, Jed and Erik, with C.J. Stratford behind them, surreptitiously. They went straight to the first item on the agenda — the no-confidence vote.

The Chairman of the Board, Emanuel Borden, looked at Connor questioningly and then at the woman behind him.

A soft whisper came from behind Connor. "Say nothing. Let them put both their feet in it."

With a tremor of trepidation, Connor took a breath and shook his head at Borden.

They read off the 'charges', the reasons for their decision to take such a drastic step.

Connor's stomach churned as each was read, many of them having more to do with his lifestyle than with his ability or inability to run the company, discounting his degrees or his years with the OI, ending with a statement of opprobrium regarding the spending of corporate money on the party celebrating his rise to C.E.O.

Anger rising, he wanted to protest but a slender hand on his arm prevented him.

Glancing back at the woman behind him, her eyes unreadable behind the slightly tinted glasses, he knew he was putting a lot of trust in her. A part of him worried about that. A lot.

Surprised at his silence, Borden said, "Then let's call the vote."

A few eyes looked down the table at Connor, frowning, wondering what he was up to. Including Marc Warren, who scowled past his shoulder at the woman sitting behind him.

One or two seemed concerned, another looked frankly worried and several of them looked angry.

The vote went around the table and Connor marked each of those who voted against him in his head. It wasn't as sure a thing as he had feared, the vote was nearly fifty-fifty, six for, five against, one of the six had been shaky, another abstaining, both the last two giving Connor an apologetic look. It was clear that the abstention was a surprise to one or two of the people there.

From behind him a soft voice spoke as she got to her feet, laying a hand consolingly on his shoulder. "Now you know who your friends are, Mr. O'Donnell. And there are more of them than you and the opposition thought."

It was an encouraging thought, as were the faces of those who had fought his ouster.

She stood, stepped past him, looking over those at the table.

"You've recorded the vote?" she asked, her eyes going to the secretary, who gave her a look like a deer in the headlights.

Recorded but not certified.

The woman nodded.

Several members of the Board stiffened in concern at the question. She was asking whether their votes were a matter of record.

With a cool smile, C.J. Stratford looked at them.

"First, I want it recorded that this vote in and of itself was illegal and improper. This is not a publicly owned company, although many of you have a vested interest in it. Even if it were the corporate bylaws state clearly that it is to be run in concordance with the late *founder's* will. That would be the first Connor O'Donnell, not the recently deceased Brian or his father Owen. Based on that will this Board was always and ever intended to be no more than an *advisory* board, not one of management. Unfortunately, the previous Mr. O'Donnell felt the need to rely increasingly on the Board far more than perhaps he should have during his nearly twenty-year tenure, giving it extraordinary power and so custom prevailed, leading us to this moment. Custom does not carry in corporate law. Therefore, you cannot either as a body or individually censure Mr. O'Donnell in any way, shape or form."

That was clearly news to Marc Warren. He looked poleaxed and then glared at one of his subordinates in fury…and concern. Someone hadn't done their research.

"There are some who might debate the validity of this statement. I welcome them to reread the terms of the original wills and the contracts they signed when taking their positions."

She gestured to the envelopes. Her gaze swept across those in the room. She smiled a little coldly.

"In light of that and any potential lawsuits that may be brought with the intention of enforcing this no-confidence vote, I'm going to advise Mr. O'Donnell to sue the Board as an entity and each of you who voted negatively individually as well. He should also cut off your stipends for serving on this Board, as you are no longer working in the best interests of the company and its Chief Executive Officer, Mr. O'Donnell, as such a proxy fight would be to the detriment of the company. As CEO and sole heir, he has that power. Mr. Warren and many of the attorneys for the corporation would also be enjoined from assisting in those lawsuits due to their involvement with the company, their obligation there and their involvement in the current situation. It would be a clear conflict of interest."

A tremor went through the room, alarm sparking among those present.

That kind of litigation could tie them all up in court for years and it would be hugely expensive. With Warren forced to recuse himself, their biggest gun would also be silenced.

"Oh and to correct a misconception… Mr. O'Donnell paid for the celebratory party out of corporate funds and he was well within his rights to do so, since many of the company's most active clients attended, therefore it was as much a business event as a personal one."

She glanced at the Chairman. "It might be advisable to reconsider both your position and your proposal before committing yourself any further to either. I would also advise that should any word of this leak out and therefore damage the reputation of the company that you personally should be held responsible for allowing it to continue."

Then she stepped back, once again taking her seat behind Connor.

Connor looked at the stunned faces of those seated at the table and restrained a smile. She had definitely tossed a fox into the henhouse.

As they debated it among themselves, Connor turned in his seat.

"Were you there?" he asked, curiously. "At the party?"

He didn't remember her being there.

"The party?" Amused, she looked at him and answered honestly. "I wasn't invited, Mr. O'Donnell."

He winced a little. He had invited most of the upper echelons, expecting — quite rightly — that few would attend.

One or two members of the Board were still arguing vehemently in low voices that they could still oust him and Connor marked them for removal at the earliest opportunity.

Knowing those individuals involved, he suspected they had seen a chance to change their financial status from advisory stipend to paid members of a controlling board in his absence. Voting themselves an increase in pay would have been relatively easy at that point, perhaps even a share of the profits. Many companies worked that way.

In the end, though, the recommendation was made that an apology be tendered for the actions of the Board, the motion was tabled and the meeting declared closed.

The members who had supported him surrounded him, shaking his hand as Monaghan's staff came in to silently clear the remains of the Board Members lunch.

"Nothing against your father, Connor," one of them said, "he was a good man but we needed some new blood here. I tried to tell them that. You can't run a business well by committee."

And it hadn't been. As much as Connor had loved his father they all knew that.

The same man nodded toward Erik and Jed.

"New ideas, new directions, or fade and die as so many other companies have in this economy. You've brought some good people in."

It gave not just Connor, but Jed and Erik a boost to hear it, heartening Connor a little.

The sixth nay-voting member came up to apologize personally for voting in the negative.

"Sorry, Connor," he said, offering his hand. "I didn't think that you had enough time to make the changes necessary but I was under a lot of pressure to vote against you."

Connor considered it before he took the offered hand. "Bill, you owe me one."

Taking a breath, the other man nodded in acknowledgment.

When Connor turned around to thank her, C.J. Stratford was gone.

Chapter Ten

It took a little while for Connor to find her, tracking her down in the bowels of the legal section, her office little more than a slightly oversized cubicle with full walls. A file hutch took up the entire back wall, a matching desk in fake cherry cut what little remaining space there was in half. Files were stacked on a chair, a low parsons table and the floor. On the wall facing her desk was a framed picture of Denali in Alaska, the wind in the picture sending snow swirling. He'd climbed that mountain. Beside it were her diplomas. She stood bent over her desk, writing notes in a file, her firm bottom in the tight skirt and those shapely legs the first things that he saw.

She had an incredibly nice ass.

His body responded appreciatively, despite the severe suit.

"Miss Stratford?" he said, leaning a shoulder against the doorway.

She glanced back over her shoulder at him curiously. A strange sense of déjà vu went through him, reminding him of something.

"Mr. O'Donnell," she said, her eyes unreadable behind the glasses.

"I wanted to thank you for helping me," he said.

She smiled a little, her tone wry. "Just doing my job. It's what you pay me the big bucks for."

Connor had to laugh at that.

"Was there anything else?" she asked, curiously, as he continued to stand there looking at her.

By now everyone would have heard what had happened. In any business word got around quickly, as he had learned during his days in the mailroom. Several people in the small offices up and down the hall were no doubt listening to their entire conversation. It wasn't often that the big boss made his way done to this level. Connor couldn't remember ever having done so before and doubted that his father ever had.

"No," he said but he'd see that she got a promotion as well as very nice bonus in her paycheck. He needed minds like hers in this company.

Something nagged at him, though, something in the way that she stood, looking back at him over her shoulder. It was a simple, common gesture. He searched his memory.

It still bothered him when he reached his office, both Jed and Erik waiting there to celebrate his victory with bottles of champagne and smiles of relief.

With a grin, he took the proffered glass from Jed as he went to his desk.

"So, did you find her?" Jed said.

Nodding, that image of C. J. Stratford bent over her desk still haunting him, he sat back in his chair, thinking about it.

"Yes, I did."

"What did she say?" Jed asked, curious.

"That she was just doing her job," Connor said, frowning a little, considering it.

Curious himself, Connor pulled up her personnel file to put a note into it about the bonus and to learn a little more about the mysterious Miss Stratford.

Looking at the details in that file, he smiled.

Suddenly a great deal became clear, or at least clearer.

"That's not all I found."

Both Jed and Erik caught something in his voice and looked at him, intrigued.

Pressing the intercom, he said, "Beth, would you ask Miss Stratford to join us in my office? Send her right in when she arrives and hold my calls. We're going to take a little time to celebrate. You should celebrate, too. Go home once you let Miss Stratford in. We'll be having her to dinner. Go enjoy your family."

"Yes, sir!"

Since most nights he worked late, sometimes so did she, so it was an unexpected and welcome bonus.

He looked at Jed and Erik, who both looked mystified.

"It seems only fair that Miss Stratford joins the celebration," Connor explained, lifting his glass before sipping at the champagne, settling back with satisfaction. "We'll need another glass, Jed."

Obediently, Jed went to get one from the bar.

A few moments later the door to Connor's office opened and C.J. Stratford walked in, looking all prim, proper, buttoned up and corporate in her soft butter-yellow suit and horn-rimmed glasses, every hair neatly in place.

Smiling, Connor shoved out of his chair, taking the extra glass as Jed handed it to him and walked across the office to greet her.

"Hello, Cherry," he said, offering her the glass.

Jed and Erik went still. They turned to look at her, each of them starting to grin.

Grinning back a little uncertainly, Cherry pulled her glasses off to look at him, then Jed and Erik, taking the flute of champagne Connor offered as he went past.

"I wasn't certain whether you recognized me or not. What gave me away?"

Connor remembered making love to her in the bathroom that last day, the way she had turned her head to look at him over her shoulder as he fucked her… The memory made him go hot and hard all over again.

"The way you were bent over your desk," Connor said, as he went to lock the door of his office, just in case. He didn't want any interruptions. "If I remember right I took you that way that last day. Why didn't you tell me who you were?"

A burst of heat went through her at his words, remembering.

It had given her a pang each time Cherry had seen him, Jed or Erik in the halls, knowing they didn't recognize her, watching them walk away but there had been nothing she could do. She'd had to play it out.

Just looking at them hurt. She wanted to touch them so bad. She wanted them to touch her even more.

Sipping her champagne, her heart thudding slowly, heavily, she watched Connor walk back toward her.

"I didn't know if you wanted me to," she said, walking toward the windows, not looking at any of them. "And, I couldn't. If anyone knew of our relationship, however brief, it would have called into question my ability to represent you. You would have had to hire an attorney. It would have taken time. Time that would have cost you, entrenched the Board in power, and hurt OI."

There was also the question of how they had met, which would have made it impossible for her to defend him. Nor could she have revealed to whatever attorney he did hire what she knew of internal company business as that was in her own contract.

Ethically, it was still questionable, but she could live with that.

Both answers rendered Connor silent. He heard the undercurrent of pain in her voice. Now he understood why she had lied to him at the Board meeting. If anyone had overheard…

"So," she asked, puzzled, "I thought we had everything straightened out. Why did you call me here when we already talked down in my office?"

"Why did you leave?" Connor asked.

Both of them knew what he was really asking.

"No one asked me to stay," she said simply.

They had asked the first morning, but they hadn't the second.

It wasn't the answer Connor had expected.

He winced. It stung.

Considering all that happened between them, all that they had done to and with her that must have hurt.

Looking at Jed and Erik he could see that neither of them had thought of it either. So simple. None of them had thought to ask her to stay. Just stay.

"How did we miss that?" he asked them.

Both shook their heads.

"And I couldn't anyway. I'd been hearing rumors about the no-confidence vote, nothing concrete, nothing at least until you were confirmed as C.E.O.," she continued. "I tried to stop it, but no one would listen to me. If I had told you about it, though, if anyone knew about our relationship, I couldn't defend you against it. I would have had to recuse myself. So, I had to stay away."

That she had known and tried to stop it, though, had fought for him despite everything, despite everything... or because of it.

He hadn't done this well.

She was the playmate, the lover for whom they had been looking.

But he could fix that.

Reaching for the pins in her hair, tugging them free, his voice soft, Connor said, "Cherry, please stay…"

Cherry took a breath. It had been so odd not to have any of them touching her. Her heart ached more than a little, seeing them all this close again, smelling Connor's cologne, remembering what it had been like to touch them, to fuck them.

The flow of words in her head came to an abrupt stop as her breath caught and she realized what he had just said. "What?"

"Stay," he repeated, smiling, pulling one pin after another from her hair so that it spilled down over shoulders. "We all want you. All three of us, Jed, Erik…me."

Cherry looked up into his brilliant blue eyes. Her heart seemed to stop beating.

Then suddenly sense took over.

"Wait a minute," she said and stuck her arm out, narrowing her eyes.

Her arm came up against a strong solid male chest, the muscles flexing beneath her hand. It was an incredible sensation. Her heart stuttered as her pussy went tight.

"There are going to be some rules this time."

Giving her a look, grinning at the challenge, Connor tried to go around her. She stayed with him, though, like a guard for the NBA even in her heels, fighting a smile.

"This time, I'm not the only one naked most of the time. You all have gorgeous bodies, I want to touch and play, too."

Almost too late, she saw Connor's eyes shift, nearly forgetting Jed and Erik behind her. She spun.

Jed caught at her suit jacket but she let her arms slide out of it as she turned to plant a hand in the center of his lean chest before dodging away from him, too, giving him a warning look. It was like trying to hold back a muscular wall.

"That goes for you, too, Jed, Erik," Cherry said, fighting laughter. "Nope. This time, I get my fun, too. You first. Strip. All three of you."

Gesturing, doing a good imitation of chicken-necking, gesturing at her body, she said, "You ain't touchin' this 'til you do."

"It's three against one," Connor pointed out, clearly amused but he loosened his tie.

Erik stepped in her way. She braced a hand against his chest, narrowing her eyes at him, the solid muscle of him hard beneath her hand. Like she could stop him…

"You heard me, mister," she said, narrowing her eyes at him. "You, too."

Fighting a grin, Erik started to comply but then made a grab at her wrist.

Laughing, she danced away from him, evading Connor's grab at the same time, ducking around to the other side of the conference table.

"I can keep this up all night," she said, circling behind the table, grinning. "Strip, gentlemen."

With a glance at Jed and a nod, tilting his head at Jed to tell him to circle around, Connor draped his suit jacket over a chair, moving slowly toward the end of the conference table as he unbuttoned his cuffs. He couldn't help smiling as he unbuttoned his shirt, giving Erik a significant look.

Erik nodded.

This was going to be fun.

His green eyes twinkling, moving to stand and block her exit from that end of the table, Erik shrugged out of his jacket, too, hanging it over one of the conference chairs.

On the other side of the table Jed, grinning, tossed his jacket carelessly over a chair, tugging his shirttails free, unbuttoning his cuffs as well as he, too, circled her, going in support of Connor.

Shots of excitement burst through Cherry as she watched them surround her, close in on her, even as they undressed.

God, they were beautiful.

Her heart pounded — 'Cherry, please stay' kept echoing through her head — and her pussy ached, moisture gathering between her thighs.

Connor O'Donnell wasn't a man to say please much.

More and more of his magnificent chest became visible as he, too, tugged his shirttails free. Her nipples tightened, chafing at her bra beneath her shirt as she watched.

Jed's leaner, tauter body, was too distracting, so gorgeous, the muscles tight, smooth and flat, becoming visible as his shirt parted.

Her mouth started to water.

They were closing too fast but she thought she might have a way to slow them down.

Backing toward the windows, eyeing Erik warily, she said, "Just to be fair…"

She unbuttoned her own cuffs, watching them circle and close around her as she unbuttoned her shirt, biting her lip a little. It was a race against time.

For a moment, Connor was transfixed, slowing his pace as the buttons of Cherry's shirt parted one by one and the mounds of her breasts, tightly constrained, pushed upward and a little together, were exposed.

His hardening cock stiffened further as her fingers plucked shakily at the buttons of her shirt and it opened further to reveal what she wore underneath the buttoned-down shirt.

His body tightened.

The bustier was of figured yellow satin, bound tightly around her body to push her breasts up and together, a thin scrap of paler yellow cotton at the top of each tiny cup covering the dusky shadow of her nipples. Watching him, them, Cherry ran her hands over her breasts, pushing them together, caressing them, the hardened nipples peaking beneath the thin cotton as she teased them by pinching and flicking them with her fingers.

Connor's mouth went hot and dry, his cock coming to rigid attention.

It was wonderfully, incredibly erotic for Cherry to touch and play with herself as they watched.

She saw Connor's blue eyes go smoky and hot, Jed shifting a little to resettle himself as Erik groaned and she smiled at their expressions.

By now even Erik had his shirt open, revealing the broad strong muscles of his massive chest.

Looking at the three of them with their shirts unbuttoned, their torsos exposed, all so gorgeous, each different, she didn't think she'd ever seen anything sexier, anything more beautiful. There was definitely something about a half-naked man. Her breath caught, even as she reached behind her to the button of her skirt.

She had their undivided attention now as the movement pushed her chest forward, reminding them of the time they'd kept her bound.

With a smile, she unbuttoned the button, sliding the zipper down with a soft purring sound, letting the skirt drop to puddle at her feet so that she stood in just her opened white button-down shirt and what was beneath it.

"Sweet Jesus," Jed said, stopped in his tracks.

All the air left his lungs.

It was the sexiest thing he had ever seen outside of a magazine.

Beneath the tight bustier she wore a yellow garter belt to hold up the lace-topped silk stockings on her shapely legs, made shapelier by the three-inch heels she wore and a pair of yellow lace boy-shorts, cut to expose the white globes of her firm round ass.

Looking from one to the other of them, curling her hands beneath the tiny cups of the bustier, she pushed her breasts higher, playing with her nipples, scraping her fingernails lightly over the cotton covering them.

Jed thought he'd lose his mind as he watched.

Connor's cock went as hard as rock, looking at her.

She looked like a model for one of the better men's magazines except that she stood in front of them.

Erik groaned.

Turning her head, she looked at him, smiling.

In one quick motion Connor had her wrist, a sharp tug yanking her carelessly over his shoulder as she squealed with surprise.

Laughing, she said, "Connor, put me down."

Resolutely, he carried her toward his private elevator. His now for certain, thanks to her. He thought they should show her his, their, appreciation.

"Someone needs a spanking, Jed, don't you think?" he said, as Jed and Erik fell in beside him. "First for leaving without saying goodbye and second for being a tease."

With a grin, Jed said, "I do."

Her bottom was there in front of him, the firm white globes exposed by the thin lace boy shorts and available.

"Jed," Cherry said, warningly, looking at him from beneath her hair. "No."

His hand cracked sharply across one rounded mound.

The stinging pain made her squeak but there was something oddly exciting about it, too.

"Jed," she cried.

"I'm not done, that was for leaving," he drawled and dealt her another resounding smack on her other cheek, hard enough to leave her pretty white ass pink and glowing. "That was for teasing."

That time she actually yelped but she didn't look as if she minded that much, Jed noticed.

Now both of her ass cheeks showed the evidence of his fingers. He smoothed his hand over those smooth white globes.

Turning to give Erik a shot, Connor said, "Erik?"

A big hand cracked against her bottom, she grunted and gasped. Warmth flooded her, both her bottom and her pussy.

She wriggled as Connor pushed the button for his private elevator. The door slid silently open.

Erik spanked her other ass cheek hard. He smoothed a hand over her warmed buttocks. Her pussy flooded, drenching the lace. Heat and anticipation were pouring through her.

"Connor," Cherry said, wiggling, "Put me down."

As the doors slid shut he did, letting her slide from his shoulder into the center of their private circle, looking from Jed to Erik.

Cherry found herself looking up, tightly hemmed in by three magnificent men, all pressing close. She raised her eyes to Connor's blue ones, glancing over each shoulder to find Erik and Jed to each side of her. Their shirts were all open. In delight, she ran her hands over them, almost overwhelmed by their maleness, the sheer level of testosterone in such a small space intoxicating.

Her clear delight in touching them was exhilarating.

Deliberately, as the elevator rose all three set about removing their dress slacks.

They couldn't keep their hands off her, either.

Or their cocks, bumping them against her hips, her belly, her ass, leaving cool dots of pre-cum on her skin. Her hands danced over them, sleeking up the silky skin over the rigid muscle beneath. They were delightfully hard beneath her hands.

All three of them were running their hands over her, as well, brushing and teasing her nipples beneath the thin cotton covering them, tweaking, teasing and plucking at them until they were as hard as pebbles, sliding their hands over her smooth bottom and between her thighs, over her mound to tease at her clit beneath the lace.

Still… Cherry didn't want to make it too easy for them.

The elevator bounced a little and the doors whispered open.

With a grin, she darted out.

She didn't expect Erik's quickness this time. He snared her wrist as she slipped through, swinging her around with her back against his broad chest. In one smooth motion he bent quickly, wrapped his arms over hers, underneath and around her thighs and lifted her from the floor.

Cherry's back collided with a hard male body as she gasped, finding herself suspended in the air, Erik's arms wrapped firmly around her legs so that she was pinned against his chest, her arms trapped beneath his. She was helpless, her thighs open to reveal her pussy and the drenched lace.

"You're not getting away this time," he said with a smile.

"Erik," she gasped, half in surprise, half in amazement.

It was an interesting view, Cherry wearing that bustier, locked in Erik's arms with her legs spread.

"How long can you hold her like that, big guy?" Connor asked, curiously.

Erik lifted an eyebrow and curled his arms a little, lifting her higher. "I bench five hundred pounds, Conn, you know that. She's a little thing, she weighs nothing. In this position?"

He shrugged carelessly.

Stepping closer Connor looked Cherry in the eye and grinned.

"Check," Connor said, hooking his fingers in the thin cotton covering her nipples, "and mate."

Her breath caught, her blue eyes going wide…and hot.

Connor yanked down the thin cotton, revealing her deep pink areole, the nipples already as hard as pebbles. Reaching into the cups to lift her breasts out, he tweaked her hard nubs, watching her blue eyes go smoky, her lips part. Deliberately, he lowered his head to one and bit it.

She jolted and he smiled.

"Hey, Jed," Connor said, "do you want some of this?" He looked at Erik. "Do you mind?"

With his swelling cock not far below Cherry's tight ass, brushing against the wetness drenching the lace at her pussy, Erik shook his head. He didn't mind at all, her soft scent rose to him, a combination of her perfume and the sweet aroma of her arousal.

"Not at all. Help yourself," he said, shifting his hips to rub the crown of his shaft against her wet entrance.

"Hey," Cherry said, in protest.

They ignored her.

"Don't mind if I do," Jed said, "but I'm hungry for pussy. I haven't had any for weeks."

Not since she had left them.

Cherry shivered in anticipation.

"By all means," Connor said, stepping away, gesturing as Erik easily hefted Cherry higher, spreading her legs even further apart.

Exposed and captive once again, Cherry tried to wriggle free but Erik had her securely held. She could barely move.

Smiling, Jed stepped closer to run his hands over the lace covering her pussy, pausing to toss his slacks over the back of the couch.

Connor lowered his head to her nipple and nipped it.

She moaned.

Jed tugged on her lace panties. There was a snick. She opened her eyes to see him holding his penknife in his hand. With his brown eyes on hers, he slipped the blade beneath the lace at her pubic bone. She felt the cold metal of the knife against her skin and gasped as he sawed lightly at it. The lace parted at pressure from the blade, whispering open with soft pops. He drew the lace away, exposing her.

"Sorry, Cherry," Jed said, "but you look too fetching in those stockings and these are in my way."

Cool air blew against her hot pussy.

Cherry shivered with anticipation, thinking of his mouth on her, his tongue inside her.

Jed slid his fingers between her thighs to dip a little into her, playing at her entrance.

"So wet," he whispered, his fingers teasing. "And so hot."

She was. He plundered between her thighs, swirling his fingers between her nether lips. It was sweet to touch her once again.

"You know," he said, almost idly, "I really do like to eat pussy."

She moaned.

He kissed her gently beside her eye, brushed another across her lips.

"And I love to hear you scream."

He settled on the end of the arm of the couch, just the right height for where Erik held her suspended.

"Jed," she whispered, in anticipation.

Already moisture flooded her labia as they blushed a deeper pink.

"That's so beautiful," he said, with a sigh, admiring the view.

Sliding his arms under her thighs to give Erik a little help, a little extra support, Jed angled her hips a little.

Looking up, he met her blue eyes.

"Cherry," he said, with a smile and lowered his mouth to her pussy, taking one long, very slow, very deep lick along her slit.

Licking and lapping, spearing his tongue deeply into her, dancing it around the nub of her clit, Jed drank her in, listening in delight to her moans as he ravished her with his mouth and she drenched him in her fluids. He drowned in the scent of her, the taste of her. He found her clit with his thumb, teasing and tormenting it as he lapped at her, the scent of her musk rising around him, the taste of her rich. Sliding the middle finger of one hand into her soaking pussy, he coated it in her juices.

Listening to the soft cries in her throat, to that spiraling wail, Jed wanted to hear her beg, wanted to know that she was theirs.

"Tell me what you want…"

A moan. "Please, god, Jed."

Pleasure poured through her, taking all the strength, all the fight out of her. Cherry let her head fall back against Erik's shoulder as she let out a soft groan, pleasure tightening her belly. Erik's cock bumped teasingly against her ass, against the tight opening there as Jed feasted on her, his tongue diving in and out of her, fucking her deeply with it. It was delicious, delirious. Her hands clenched over Erik's arms, clinging to him as Jed devoured her. Her hips bucked, her pussy pulsing, aching.

Connor suckled hard on her breast, drawing her nipple into his mouth, nipping and biting. He curled his hand around the other, pinching her other nipple tightly as her breasts swelled against his mouth and hand.

She moaned, unable to writhe, unable to escape Jed's relentless tongue, Connor's mouth and teeth, locked immobile in Erik's arms. Her nipples were taut and aching as sharp spears of pleasure lanced through her

Pleasure blinded her, her body trembling as delight shot through her body like lightning from Connor's mouth, teeth and hands on her, brilliant bursts of it rolling through her, gathering with each brush of Jed's thumb on her clit, to the deeper ecstasy of his tongue sucking her, licking her, fucking her. He drove her up, holding her there, trembling, needing…

God, she had missed this, she had missed them. She trembled and yet still she wanted more. She wanted them. All of them. One at a time or all at once. Again and again.

Cupping her hips, Jed tilted her, one thumb working her, sliding his finger up into her ass and then he devoured her, sucking and licking at her clit.

She came with a scream, the orgasm bursting through her like fireworks, exploding behind her eyes, fire racing through her veins, scorching beneath her skin. It was as if she were on fire, as if she had suddenly burst into flame, her body locking as it took her, turning her mindless, helpless, shuddering wildly as his mouth worked on her.

Jed looked at Erik. "Still good?"

Erik was fine. He just couldn't speak.

Cherry's weight was nothing, the feel of her in his arms was great. It was the juices from her dripping flexing pussy coating his rock-hard cock that drove him crazy. It was the head of his cock brushing across her tight heat and the even tighter sphincter of her ass that had him speechless. Remembering how incredibly tight her ass was, his cock was so hard it throbbed. He just wanted to fuck her every which way until she couldn't stand, ramming his thick shaft into her again and again.

Erik, breathing heavily to keep from fucking her where they stood, nodded.

All of three of them were hard as rocks, eager to fuck her until she couldn't stand or walk so she couldn't leave them again.

Connor watched her blue eyes darken and haze again, brushing the golden hair back from her face.

He cupped her cheek, waiting until her eyelids fluttered, her eyes focused on him.

"We missed you," he said and watched her lovely eyes widen. "I missed you."

He looked at Jed and Erik.

"Bedroom?" he asked.

Wiping his mouth with his shirttail and grinning, Jed nodded. "God, she's incredible."

"How fast can you make her come?" Connor asked, as they reached the bedroom. He had an idea.

"Cherry?" Jed said, "As responsive as she is? Like a rocket."

With look at Jed and a nod at Erik, Connor said, "Do it. Tag team, old buddy, tag team."

Turning Connor looked at Erik, seeing the tension, the desire, the pure need in his friend's face, Cherry still spread in his arms.

"Take her."

They were going to tag-team her, one of them fucking her while the other two recovered.

Erik let his head fall back in relief, his cock sliding against her sweet, hot, drenched pussy, wetting him even further. That wasn't what he wanted, though. He had waited for this. He lifted her, his oak hard cock rising automatically into position, and lowered her slowly onto the rounded head of it, impaling her ass on him. His hips thrust up, driving his cock into her snug little hole as his hands pushed her down.

She was as tight as he remembered. Erik nearly couldn't stand it, she was so very close around his throbbing cock.

He sat on the edge of the bed and she dropped another inch onto him. It was wonderful. The juices from her dripping pussy lubricated him even more.

Carefully, he lifted her up a little to spread it around a little. She moaned as he drove her down on him again. Wrapping his legs around hers, he drew her legs farther apart for Jed again before settling his own hands on her hips to press her even further down as she sank onto him deliciously.

She was so tight, so incredibly tight it was nearly painful but each motion was like having his cock stroked, pumped.

The thick length of Erik forced a deep guttural groan out of her, the fullness of him inside her incredible. Cherry let her head fall back against his shoulder. It was fantastic.

Driving two fingers up inside her, Jed spread her thighs, suckling hard and fast on her clit, her body going rigid, her back arching as Erik drove his shaft deeper into her.

Pleasure surged through her again.

Free now, Connor's hands closed around her breasts, squeezing hard, nearly crushing them and she arched into them.

Then Jed nibbled lightly on her clit and her body bucked, pleasure building as he drew hard on her stroking deep within her.

Kneeling beside them on the bed, Connor fisted his cock.

"Cherry," Connor said, "suck me."

He was so hard at the thought of what they were going to do to her.

Blindly, she reached for him, closed her hand around his rigid member and turned her head to take his cock, opening her mouth to take him like a baby bird for food. That shot a bolt of desire straight into his iron-hard cock. Her hot wet mouth closed around him and he almost lost his mind.

He slid a hand into her hair, cupping her head so he could keep fucking her sweet mouth as Erik thrust up into her.

Connor and Jed, seeing it, knew he was coming. Jed suckled her, finger-fucking her fast and hard.

Muffled by Connor's cock deep in her mouth, Cherry screamed as her orgasm took her. The vibration was nearly more than Connor could bear. Jed lunged up her body to plunge his cock into her pussy, his hand on her shoulder as he rammed into her, fucking her hard

With a deep rumbling groan, Erik erupted.

Connor heard Jed groan, too. Locking his hands around Cherry's head, he drew his cock back enough for her to get some air before driving it deep into her mouth, into her throat, he and Jed coming nearly simultaneously inside her.

Suddenly Cherry was filled, completely, being fucked by all three men, every orifice of her body filled with them again, as Erik squeezed her breasts tightly with each increasingly wild thrust. Another orgasm gathered as all three of them fucked her, as all three of them came, Jed's cock and Erik's rubbing her between them.

Her mind went blank as ecstasy erased it, her body bucked uncontrollably, pleasure roaring through her as they fucked her hard and deep, thick rigid cocks ramming into her again and again.

The hot gush of Jed's cum bathed her pussy as Connor's filled her mouth, jetting against the back of her throat. She swallowed him as quickly as she could, what part of her mind that still remained aware determined to take all of him.

Connor shivered as she drank him, swallowing as he gushed into her. He watched her, her eyes closed, her throat working as she tried to take everything he could give her, one arm sliding around his hips to take him deeper.

Both Jed and Erik looked ecstatic, both still pumping into her as she trembled and shook between them.

Reluctantly he withdrew his cock from her mouth as she murmured in dismay, sucking lightly at him as he went.

That was nice.

Wearily, content, Jed shifted a little to the side, to a similar protest from Cherry as he withdrew from her.

With an evident effort, Erik pushed them carefully back on the bed with his legs, one arm locked around Cherry, his cock still imbedded in Cherry's ass.

His knees going weak, Connor followed and sagged against the headboard next to them as Jed did the same, flopping down on Erik's left.

Cherry had collapsed, too, no surprise.

He looked at her splayed limply across Erik's broad chest, her golden hair disheveled once again and tumbled. Her blue eyes were closed and she was breathing hard but she looked sated, happy.

So was he.

He smiled as he stroked her breast idly. There were marks on it from Erik's fingers. Connor didn't think Cherry minded much. She had one arm now around Jed and her other reached for Connor.

Connor had no objection to that touch at all as he stretched out beside them to prop his head up on his hand, nuzzling her breast as she stroked his hair, the gentle touch soothing. It stirred things in him that he had been too busy to feel for a long time.

It had been a good plan but like all battle plans it hadn't quite worked the way they intended. Not that he had any complaints. There was still time.

"It's good to have you back, Cherry," he said, turning his head to press a kiss into her palm and saw her blue eyes soften and widen.

She took a breath and said, softly, "It's good to be back."

For a moment their eyes met and held.

There were things that you said with your friends there and things that you didn't. He would find a time to tell her what he felt and he suspected Jed and Erik would, too. Each in their own way.

He smiled. They were keeping her.

"Are you all right, Erik?" Cherry whispered, her throat too dry and hoarse for anything else.

At the sound, Jed glanced at Connor, and then went to fetch some drinks and snacks.

Erik shifted her a little, his hands settling onto her belly.

"Um-hmmm," he murmured contentedly. "Everyone keeps asking me that. I like the weight of you on top of me."

They had a picnic on the bed, with champagne and caviar, a little pâté de foie gras and crackers.

Cherry just shook her head at the selection and grinned.

"So, what's your favorite fantasy, Cherry?" Connor asked, idly playing with her nipple. He needed to know just how adventurous she could be but he was pretty certain he already knew.

She turned her head to look at him. "Besides this?"

Connor smiled.

"Was this a fantasy of yours?" Jed asked, curiously.

"To be dessert, spread out on display? Oh, yes!" she sighed with delight. "I had read about the Romans doing something like it and wondered what it would be like to have someone eat from me. Much less eat me, especially so thoroughly and well."

She looked at Jed and grinned.

It was hard for any of them not to remember how incredible she had looked, how enticing. Or how sweet she had tasted.

Connor thought he'd have to ask for a repeat performance. A private repeat performance, just for the four of them.

"A ménage a trois was another, although I would have settled happily for just one of you, if I had to," she said, smiling wryly at all of them, "Three such gorgeous ones? A ménage a quatre? That doesn't even enter into the realm of fantasy."

They all grinned, Connor kissing her shoulder lightly.

"So," Connor prompted, "Second?"

Frowning a little as she considered it, she said, "Not second. Just different…being carried off into the woods, bound, naked and at the mercy of my captors, who then fuck me every which way whenever they wish, out in the open under the stars."

Jed's eyes lit up.

That was his particular fantasy. He hadn't even dared hope, until they met Cherry.

Now?

"Led with a collar? While one or the other of us covers you like a stallion does a mare?"

It was clear she'd never thought of that before but she was definitely thinking about it now.

Jed looked at Connor and Erik, back to Cherry, his heart racing. He'd practically grown up on his grandparent's ranch until Jed's father had been transferred. The three of them had spent parts of a lot of summers there. He still went back now and then. That one particular fantasy had always been in the back of his mind.

Just the thought of the idea sent a shot of excitement through all of them.

It was easy to picture, a collar around Cherry's slender throat as they each took her from behind.

Connor glanced at Erik, who was also getting hot and hard at the thought.

"That could be arranged," Connor said, considering the logistics. Cherry definitely had a definite sense of adventure.

"Short term?" she continued, "Having someone who thinks I'm so hot he has to bend me over and fuck me just because he's hot for me."

"Will two or three of us do?" Connor asked, looking at his friends.

Jed grinned, stroking her belly as Erik's eyes lit up.

"By preference," she said, smiling at him. "What about you?"

"Riding to a motorcycle rally with Jed and Erik, a hot sexy blonde with a truly gorgeous body on the back of my bike," Connor said, his eyes fixed on her. "Having her peel slowly out of her gear down to a tiny pair of shorts and a tie-top, passing her back and forth between us when we camp at night, loving every moment of it while folks wonder if she's fucking all three of us."

A breath shuddered out of her.

"You do like motorcycles?" he asked, as he saw her eyes light up.

"I have my endorsement and my own bike," she said, "but I don't mind riding two up."

He should have known, beneath the business suit beat the heart of a biker babe. Connor smiled at the thought.

Erik chuckled, "We noticed."

She elbowed him and grinned.

Connor buried his mouth in the curve of her elbow, Cherry quivering at the touch as he thought about the next rally, going hot, hearing her cries of pleasure in his head, or seeing her bent over, while he ran a hand over her flank, ready to use her as soon as Jed finished. Ride her hard, put her away wet and satisfied.

They looked at Erik.

"I compete in Strong man contests," he said. "My fantasy has always been being able to fuck a woman as we fucked Cherry today, me holding her, fucking her up the ass as you, Conn, or Jed, fuck her, taking our pleasure of her. I would love to see Jed eat

Cherry as she screams on my cock, then either or both of you fucking her while I hold her for your pleasure until I come myself."

All of them shuddered.

"Can you hold her and fuck her pussy while Jed or I fuck her ass?" Connor asked.

Cherry looked to Erik, who grinned.

"It would be fun to try," Erik said. "Can we do that as well?"

With a glance at Cherry, her eyes glowing, color flooding her cheeks as Erik quickly lifted her, Connor said, "Definitely. Want to practice?"

His cock already hard, Erik surged to his feet, impaling Cherry on it even as he stood. She cried out to find the thick length of him so deep inside her so suddenly, so completely, his big hands cupped around her tight ass, spreading her cheeks for the other two.

Jed handed Connor the lube with a smile.

They had the advantage of already having come, so they could make this last, they could fuck her blind.

Stepping into her line of sight, Connor lubed himself thoroughly, making sure that she saw how hard and thick he was. He thought of Jed's description of the stallion covering the mare, stepped behind her and thrust into her ass hard and fast, his hands on her shoulders as she arched, a moan bursting out of her.

It was incredible, holding back, holding onto control, Connor watching Jed take her ass next, until she and he were almost there and then pulling out so that Connor could take his turn again, until both of them were almost painfully hard and she was nearly sobbing with need.

He nearly staggered as he stepped away from her, Jed taking his place, determined to do him one better, one stallion to another. He pounded into her.

They fucked her hard but Connor harder, Erik visibly struggling for control as Connor thrust and shifted while Cherry moaned and groaned between them, pleasure building. She shuddered. Then Connor withdrew and Jed was inside her, then Connor, taking their turns doing her. This time truly tag-teaming her, making it last. Wallowing in her. It was glorious, incredible.

She cried out with pleasure nearly constantly, her body shivering and quivering in their arms, her head thrown back in ecstasy as they took her again and again.

It was mindboggling, mind-blowing, to have first Connor and then Jed driving into her, listening to their groans as they shafted her, as they fucked her.

Jed's was mouth against her ear, his words soft, tight and intent as his hips slammed against her. "Ours. To claim. To take. And mine."

He erupted inside her, gushing, bursting, his body rigid as she cried out, her body pushing back to take him deeper inside her.

Connor drove up into her, so hot, so hard, pulsing and then he poured into her, erupting, sending his hot cum deep into her.

With a deep growl, Erik came, too, finally jetting into her tight, hot pussy.

Limp, exhausted, their fluids filling her, dripping out of her, Cherry was completely unable to move, laying her head on Erik's broad chest as he eased them both down on the bed.

This time they hadn't been saying goodbye.

Looking at her, Connor reached up to take Cherry's chin, turning her head this way and that.

"Something's missing," he said, a mock frown on his face.

A warm shaft of heat went through her.

"Connor," she breathed, knowing what he intended.

And smiled.

Holding her chin in place, Connor nodded to Erik, who pinned her wrists to each side within the circle of his big hands.

They were going to brand her, each of them laying claim to her. All three of them.

Erik's hot mouth closed over her throat first and he sucked, hard. Each hard pull on her throat drew an involuntarily moan from her, her pussy dampening as she writhed in concert with the motions of his mouth on her.

Watching Cherry's hips pump, her body shivering in pleasure at Erik's mouth on her, had its attractions. Connor looked at Jed, who grinned.

Each of them curled one of their legs over one of hers, drawing them gently apart as Erik's mouth worked on her throat.

When he finally released her, she blinked, shaking her head a little to try to clear it as Erik admired his handiwork.

Neither Connor nor Jed gave her much more time, drawing her down Erik's body so that they could both stretch against her, their mouths closing over her throat to suckle on it. She groaned, her body shuddering. Reaching down, Connor drew her leg up, reaching under it to gain access to her pussy even as Jed found her clit.

Connor slid his fingers deep into her already damp pussy as he sucked on her throat harder and harder, pumping his fingers into her.

She trembled and Jed smiled against her throat as he drew on her, his fingers playing on her clit.

Cherry moaned as her hips bucked, pleasure flooding her, groans tearing from her each time they sucked at her, their fingers both in and on her. She clutched at them, her hands fluttering like birds. She whimpered as ecstasy whipped through her again and again as they put their marks on her. It crested and she screamed her pleasure.

Both of them shifted close to her limp body, her eyelids heavy over her lovely blue eyes, Erik holding her secure.

Connor traced the livid marks on her fair skin with his finger, dropping his mouth down to kiss her gently.

"Ours," he said and she smiled.

A thrill went through her. Please stay, Cherry. All of them. All three of them.

Mine, she thought.